# DRAGON

*Also by Kaye Umansky*

The **PONGWIFFY** Series

\*    \*    \*

*More Tales from Witchway Wood*

\*    \*    \*

# The
# DREADFUL
# DRAGON

# Kaye Umansky

### Illustrated by Nick Price

BLOOMSBURY

LONDON  NEW DELHI  NEW YORK  SYDNEY

*For Mo and Ella*

Bloomsbury Publishing, London, New Delhi, New York and Sydney

First published in Great Britain in September 2012 by Bloomsbury Publishing Plc
50 Bedford Square, London, WC1B 3DP

A CIP catalogue record for this book is available from the British Library

ISBN 978 1 4088 2764 2

Typeset by Hewer Text UK Ltd, Edinburgh
Printed in Great Britain by Clays Ltd, St Ives Plc, Bungay, Suffolk

1 3 5 7 9 10 8 6 4 2

www.bloomsbury.com
www.kayeumansky.com

## Chapter One

# *Ronald in the Rain*

High in the Misty Mountains, it was raining, raining, *raining!* It rained on bushes, rocks and sheep. It rained on goats, rabbits and the odd wet wolf. It rained on everything, everywhere. But it rained *particularly* hard on the bedraggled figure toiling slowly up the slope leading to the Wizards' Clubhouse.

Ronald the Magnificent, youngest member of the Wizards' Club, was coming home. Or trying to.

'*Arrrgh . . .*' gasped Ronald. His foot came out of the mud, leaving his shoe behind. '*Oooer . . . arrrrghh . . .*'

It was lucky he had his Mystic Staff. He was using it as a kind of anchor to stop himself sliding back. He also had a decidedly un-mystic umbrella – a gift from his aunty, who was a Witch. It was small and girly, decorated with kittens and pink frills. He had to hold it at arm's length to accommodate his tall Wizard's Hat. It didn't help. The rain just poured down his sleeve and collected in his armpit.

His Cloak of Darkness was soaking up mud by the bucketful. This was a tragedy, as he hadn't even finished paying for it yet. It was top of the range. Blue velvet with a star-spangled lining. A label saying *Dry Clean Only*. Not built for mud.

'*Arrrrghhhh . . . uuuhhh . . .*'

Viciously, Ronald stabbed the Staff into the ground. It slipped. His arms wheeled, the umbrella flew up and seconds later he was flat out in a puddle, moaning softly while rain flooded his nostrils and trickled into his ears. It was his fourth puddle of the day. He was getting used to them now. He closed his eyes and decided to just lie there for a while.

It hadn't been like this earlier that morning. The sun had been shining, the birds were singing and all was well. He had set out with a light heart, intending to enjoy a pleasant stroll down to Witchway Wood. He was decked out in full Wizards' regalia – Mystic Staff, Hat of Knowledge, Robe of Mystery, Cloak of Darkness, the works – hoping to dazzle any passing admirers. Wisely, he didn't have any money on him. Some bad types lurked down in the Wood. He didn't want to be mugged by Goblins.

He hadn't taken ten paces before the sun went in, the birds shut up and it began to rain. In seconds, the trail became perilously slippery. It rained harder. When he had finally made it to the Wood, it was a deluge of mighty proportions.

The weather often did bad things when Ronald went walking. Rain, hail, thunderstorms, blizzards, you name it. This, of course, was the work of his fellow Wizards, who never treated him with respect. They were always picking on him. Hiding his hat. Teasing him about his lack of beard. Pinning joke signs on his back. Sawing down his Mystic Staff and making out he'd grown in the night. Anything for a laugh.

It had all started with his choice of name. Wizards' first names are often boringly ordinary, so it isn't surprising that they really go for it when it comes to choosing their titles. A Wizard's title should reflect his personality, special skill or general all-round brilliance.

Ronald's choice was not the best. He had blurted it out without thinking when he had first blagged his way into the Club, all set to become a Wizard because he liked the flash clothes and had heard that the sausages were good.

Wearing suit, tie and half a pot of hair gel, he had sailed in and demanded an interview. The receptionist had asked for his name and on the spur of the moment he had come out with it.

'*Ronald the Magnificent-ent-ent-ent!*' It echoed around the high rafters. It had a proud ring. Better than Ronnie Maggot, which was his real name.

The receptionist was a Zombie with brass earrings and green hair. Her name badge said BRENDA.

She stared and said, 'Oh yeah.'

The trouble was that, even on a good day, Ronald never looked magnificent. Everything on his head stuck out. Teeth, nose, ears, hair, everything. Only his chin went in, trailing off backwards into his neck. He was prone to pimples too. The home-made skin potions that his Witch aunty was always sending him stank the place out, so he just threw them away.

The receptionist (BRENDA) had asked to see his Wizard's Certificate. He didn't have one, but he lied and said it was lost in the post and he was waiting for a replacement. He spoke haughtily.

She had asked what grade he got in the exam. He said top marks, when he hadn't even *taken* an exam. His only Magical knowledge came from *My First Little Book of Wizardry*, which he had found in a second-hand book shop and hadn't even finished because it was harder than he thought.

Then came the interview with the Wizards, when the lies came so thick and fast that, by rights, his nose should have been a mile long.

When asked why he called himself Magnificent, he declared firmly that he was. Not would be one day. *Was*. When asked to demonstrate his skills, he said he'd hurt his finger. When quizzed about his relations, he said Magic ran in the family, although his dad was a plumber and his mum worked in a pie shop. He kept quiet about his Witch aunty. When asked about his reasons for wanting to join the Club, he said that he had always wanted to be a Wizard (although it actually came third, after a film star or a racing driver).

Amazingly, he had got in! In fact, they had begged him to join. Wizards know the perfect butt for jokes when they see it. From then on, it had been downhill all the way.

Of course, right now, it was uphill. In the rain.

With a groan, he sat up and spat out a mouthful of mud.

'*Blggghh! Pth, pth, ptht!*'

The rain streamed gleefully down his Hat and on to his shoulders. He struggled up, retrieved the Staff and picked up the umbrella. Two spokes were broken and it wouldn't open.

Ronald didn't care much. The umbrella was, frankly, embarrassing. But he hadn't dared to buy a new one in case he bumped into his aunty, who lived down in Witchway Wood. Knowing his luck, she would leap from behind a tree saying something like, 'Why, Ronald! A new umbrella, I see! The one I gave you not good enough?', then march him back to her cottage and force-feed him cake while lecturing him about the meaning of gratitude.

Today, there had been no sign of her. There was no sign of anybody. Anyone who had any sense was at home. Ronald had cowered miserably beneath a rain-lashed tree being laughed at by squirrels for *hours* before finally deciding to abandon ship and make a break for home.

Easier said than done. The trail was now a mudslide. It was like walking up a jelly hill. For every two steps forward, he slithered back one.

Still. Not far to go now. Last effort.

Ronald tucked the umbrella under his arm and set off again, Cloak slapping wetly around his ankles. He didn't have any socks on, so he was effectively paddling in his own shoes. This was his own fault. He had complained to Mrs Swipe, the Clubhouse laundress, about his Robe being returned with stains on. The following day, all his socks had arrived back so small that they wouldn't have fitted an Elf. He had sent off for new supplies from the Catalogue but they were refusing to let him order anything else until he paid the last instalment on the Cloak.

He rounded the final bend – and nearly wept with relief. There it was. Home!

The Wizards' Clubhouse sat at the top of a high peak. It was a fanciful affair, painted pink and gold, with turrets, towers, archways, walkways, gargoyles, statues, fountains and flags. The banners were drab and droopy with rain. The gargoyles were working overtime. The candy-coloured walls had turned an unpleasant shade of prune and the gold paint had lost its glitter. It looked like a wedding cake in a rock pool.

Ronald hurried under the archway. Right on cue, a stream of dirty water erupted from a gargoyle's mouth and poured down his neck.

'*Hwhooop*,' burped the gargoyle. 'Better out than in!'

'Thanks for that, rock head!' snarled Ronald.

'Any time, loser,' said the gargoyle. They weren't on good terms.

Ronald splashed across the courtyard through the large pool of water spreading around the base of the ornamental fountain, which was blocked with leaves.

He climbed the steps to the imposing, star-studded main door. It was fitted with a Magicom – a small, square box to one side, which communicated with Reception. The knocker was carved in the shape of a Demon's face with a letterbox mouth. Ronald lifted its heavy nose ring and knocked three times.

'*Ow!*' complained the knocker, as it always did. 'Clumsy!'

'Get over it,' snapped Ronald, as he always did, then snatched his hand away before it went for his fingers. Rain, gargoyles, knockers, they all had it in for him. No respect at all.

He waited, squelching from foot to foot, mumbling, 'Come on, come *on*!'

There came a crackling noise from the Magicom, followed by heavy breathing and the distinct sound of chewing. A bored voice said, 'Yeah?'

'It is I,' said Ronald commandingly, as a Wizard should. 'Let me in, forsooth.'

'Who?'

'I. Me.'

'Imy? Never 'eard of 'im.'

'No, *me! Me!* Ronald the Magnificent!'

'Oh.' The voice sounded deeply disappointed. 'Password?'

'*Open Sesame.*'

'Says who?'

'Says me.'

There was a pause. Ronald waited, teeth chattering. Finally, the voice came back.

'Wrong.'

'What d'you mean, wrong? Hurry up, Brenda, it's tipping it down out here.'

'Say the right password, then.'

'I *did*. It's *Open Sesame*.'

'It's changed.'

'What d'you mean? Changed to what?'

'You tell me.'

'How? I don't know what it's changed to.'

'Not my problem.'

'Who changed it? When?'

'All of 'em. Come down and told me right after you went out.'

'I suppose that's their idea of a joke,' fumed Ronald. 'I suppose they think that's funny.'

'Well, they was laughin' a lot.' There was a little pause.

'Come on, Brenda,' begged Ronald. 'You know it's me.'

'Don't. Can't see through wood, can I?'

'You know my voice, though.'

'Might be somebody else pretendin'.'

'Well, it's not. Look, this is *ridiculous*!' Ronald drew back his foot and was just about to kick the door when a voice came from behind him.

'Are you going to be long?'

## Chapter Two

# *No Respect*

A girl stood behind him. She wore a hooded cloak and stout brown boots. Over her arm was a basket covered with a checked cloth. Some peasant girl, obviously, come to sell eggs or something.

'What?' said Ronald.

'Could you stand aside, please? I'd like to get in.'

Ronald stared at her. Didn't she realise what he was? He was a Wizard. Wizards don't stand aside for anyone. He hid the umbrella behind his back and drew himself up to his full height. He was just that bit taller than she was. Good. He could speak down to her.

'Girl,' he said haughtily. 'Use the Trade Entrance. This door is for Members.'

'And you're one, are you?'

'Certainly. I am Ronald the Magnificent.'

'Well, in you go, then.'

'I'm *trying* to,' snapped Ronald. 'I'm having a little trouble.'

'In that case, shove out of the way.' The girl brushed past him, stepped up to the door and put her mouth to the Magicom.

'Hattie Crabbit,' she said briskly. 'Open up.'

To Ronald's great annoyance – with a theatrical squeak – the door swung obligingly open.

'Needs a drop of oil, that,' said the girl called Hattie Crabbit. And she strode in.

The door began to swing shut, but Ronald managed to beat it. He squeezed in just before it crashed behind him, nearly taking his hand off.

Wizards have gaudy tastes when it comes to interior decorating. The lobby was a riot of clashing colours. Red flock wallpaper, purple carpet with a swirly pattern, crystal chandeliers with black candles dribbling wax. Heavily bearded ancients scowled down from gilt-framed portraits.

A life-sized golden statue of Mervyn the Mighty, founder of the Club, stood by the door with a dramatically outflung arm. He should have held a lightning bolt, but it had snapped off and was currently propped against his feet, waiting to be fixed. He badly needed a new paint job. To add insult to injury, someone had draped a woolly scarf over his nose.

On the far side was a reception desk. Its surface was dominated by a large, jewel-encrusted spellophone. The pink receiver was shaped like a scorpion. Or a king-sized prawn. Hard to say.

Behind the desk slumped Brenda. She was chewing gum and painting her nails purple.

'Thanks,' said Hattie Crabbit, walking past and disappearing down a corridor.

'Whatever,' said Brenda, blowing a bubble and not even looking up.

'Who's that?' asked Ronald, squelching across to the desk, oozing mud at every step.

'What's it to you?'

'I'm just *asking*. Honestly. Can't I ask a polite question?'

'Take yer shoes off. Yer muckin' up the carpet.'

'I will take my shoes off,' said Ronald crossly, 'when you tell me who that girl was.'

'Old Crabbit's niece, if you must know.'

Just then, the spellophone rang. Well, it didn't exactly *ring*. Being Wizardly, it let out a high-pitched, ear-splitting shriek.

'*PICKMEUP-PICKMEUP-PICKMEUP-PICKMEUP-PICKMEUP* –'

At the same time, the dial burst into flame, spinning round like a demented Catherine wheel. This went on until Brenda picked up the receiver, trying not to smudge her nails.

'Yeah? Oh, it's you, Pauline. Nah, I ain't busy. Doin' me nails.'

'How come you let her in without a password?' demanded Ronald.

'Purple,' said Brenda down the phone, ignoring him. 'Finkin' of dyein' me hair to match.'

'I said *how come you let her in without a password?*' repeated Ronald, raising his voice.

'Yeah, I know green suits me, but I fancies a change.'

'HOW COME YOU LET HER –'

''Ang on, Pauline, I gotta deal with this nutter.' Brenda glared at Ronald and said, 'Because. Old. Crabbit. Said So. Right?'

'Well, Brenda,' said Ronald stiffly, 'I must say I am not impressed. You refuse entry to me, an actual *Member* of this club, an actual *Wizard*, just because I don't happen to have the current password, yet you let the caretaker's niece stroll in without so much as a –'

'Yeah,' said Brenda, back on the phone again. 'Yeah, there's always one.'

'Look,' shouted Ronald, 'I really think I deserve an expla—'

''Ang on a sec, Pauline.' Brenda slammed down the receiver. 'Look, I'm on the *phone*! Yer drippin' all over the place. Drop yer clothes off with Mrs Swipe.' She picked up the receiver. 'Pauline? Yeah, yer right, mad as a box of frogs . . . no, I've dealt with 'im now, he's just goin'. So. Purple, whatcha fink?'

Ronald decided to call it a day. He needed to get out of his wet clothes before he caught a chill. He turned on his heel and squelched off down the corridor, fuming.

'Put that umbrella in the bin!' ordered Brenda from behind him.

Ronald dropped the umbrella on the floor and squelched on.

'I saw that!' shouted Brenda. 'I'm tellin' yer aunty!'

Ronald dripped down the flight of stone steps that led to the Laundry. He opened the door and a great cloud of steam hit him in the face. Inside, a team of sweating girls moved around the washtubs through tumbling clouds of fog. They were watched over by Mrs Swipe, who had biceps like a wrestler, a soaked apron, a big red face and a tight little mouth.

She saw Ronald hovering in the doorway, folded her meaty arms and said, 'Oh, it's you. What now?'

'Oh – er, hello, Mrs Swipe,' said Ronald. 'I was wondering if I could drop off my things?'

'Oh, you were, were you?'

'Yes. If that's all right.'

'You couldn't 'ave put 'em outside in the basket in the proper manner first thing this morning?'

'Well – they weren't dirty then, you see. It's just that I went for a walk and . . .'

'Yes, yes, I've heard all the excuses. Pass 'em over, but don't expect 'em back until the end of the week. Just the Cloak and shoes, is it?'

'Yes. I'd – um – I'd be grateful if you'd take extra care with the Cloak. The stars on the lining . . . quite delicate, you know . . . the label says *Dry Clean Only* . . .'

'You *still* tryin' to tell me 'ow to do my job?'

'No,' said Ronald hastily. 'Certainly not, no, no. Who, me? No.'

As we have already heard, it doesn't do to upset Mrs Swipe.

Hastily, he took off the filthy Cloak and his sodden shoes, exposing his big, damp, bony feet. Mrs Swipe snatched the shoes and Cloak and slammed the door in his face. That made the third person who had been rude to him that morning, not including the gargoyle and the knocker. It was clearly going to be one of those particularly disrespectful days.

Dressed only in his Robe and Hat, arms clutched over his shivering chest, he slapped barefoot along the corridor to the next door. Behind it, he could hear the kitchen staff shouting cheerily. He pulled it open. Instantly, the conversation ceased. Maids, footmen and pastry cooks all stopped in their tracks and stared.

Butler the butler was sitting at the kitchen table in his shirtsleeves, polishing the silver. He jumped to his feet, adjusted his glasses, saw who it was and promptly sat down again.

'I say, Butler,' said Ronald into the silence.

'Yes, *sir*?' sighed Butler, polishing away. Ronald thought he detected an ironic tone in the way he said *sir*.

'I was just wondering if there was any chance of some breakfast.'

'*Breakfast?*' Butler's eyebrows shot up and disappeared into his hairline. The watching staff sniggered and twirled fingers at their heads.

'Yes,' said Ronald firmly. 'Breakfast. I'd like some.'

'Dear me, no. Oh no, no, no, *no*. Breakfast is finished. As you can see, the staff are preparing lunch.' Right on cue, the staff began clattering away, busily preparing lunch, clearly far too occupied to attend to Ronald.

'Oh, come on. Not even a sausage? I've been out walking, you see, and got delayed by rain –'

'I regret that, *sir*, I truly do. But there was a run on sausages. The proper Wizards decided to take breakfast in –'

'*What* did you just say?'

'Sorry, slip of the tongue. The *senior* Wizards took breakfast in the Lounge. The sausage platters were returned empty, as always. As were the trays of eggs, bacon, mushrooms, fried bread, black pudding, beans –'

'All right,' sighed Ronald.

'Hash-browns-toast-muffins-crumpets-pastries-ham-cheese-pickled-onions –'

'I said all *right*! I get the picture. They all stuffed themselves and left nothing for me! I get it!'

'It's good you get something, because you won't be getting breakfast at this hour,' said Butler. 'And if you don't mind my mentioning it, we don't encourage bare feet in the kitchen. This is a food preparation area. *Sir.*'

Ronald turned on his naked heel and stamped out, slamming the door behind him.

He plodded back up the steps, padded along another corridor (carpeted this time) and halted before a fancifully carved door. This was the Lounge, where the Wizards always congregated after breakfast – or before breakfast when there was something good on spellovision.

Ronald hesitated. Should he go in? The fire certainly appealed. Someone might offer him a biscuit or something, although he doubted it. Wizards are not good at sharing. On the other hand, he needed to confront them about the password and the rain. Then again, they were sure to poke fun at his feet . . .

His indecision ended when the door suddenly opened to reveal Frank the Foreteller. Frank was thin and weaselly with a ratty beard and a tatty old jumper pulled over his robe. His face lit up at the sight of Ronald.

'Aha! Young Ronald! I *knew* it would be you!'

He did too. Foreknowledge was Frank's speciality. That made him very annoying, particularly in card games when he always knew what you were about to put down.

'Yes,' said Ronald stiffly. 'I've just come back from a walk in Witchway Wood.'

'*Have* you? *Have* you indeed? Hear that, gentlemen? The lad's been walking down in the Wood. And there was I thinking he'd been skipping about on tippy-toes with the Happy Fairies in Rainbow Land!' Frank the Foreteller pointed gleefully at Ronald's unattractive feet.

'My shoes got wet in the rain,' snapped Ronald. 'Which *you* caused.'

'*Meeee?*'

'All of you. I'm not stupid, you know. I'd like to get to the fire, if you don't mind.'

'But of course! Let's get those tootsies warmed up, eh? Dave, turn the volume down. Move your feet, gentlemen, wet Wizard coming through!'

The Lounge also had red flock wallpaper and a dreadful clashing carpet, although you couldn't see much of it owing to the armchairs taking up most of the space. Their occupants sat up interestedly as Ronald stepped in, like wolves scenting prey.

The room was *hot*. A blazing fire raged in the hearth. Above, on the carved mantelpiece, was a huge, complicated clock showing the time, temperature and weather conditions in various Magical dimensions. Right now, it didn't show anything as no one had bothered to wind it up. The Wizards used it to stick junk mail behind.

As well as armchairs, there were a great many lamps, footstools and small tables heaped with newspapers, magazines, grapes, biscuits, sweets and chocolates. A large spellovision stood in one corner, tuned to a popular Gnome soap opera called *Gnome and Away*.

Getting to the fire was an obstacle course. Ronald squeezed around chairs, tripped over feet, stumbled on rugs, bumped into lamps and banged his knees on low-lying coffee tables. The Wizards watched his progress with amusement, chuckling at each little mishap. There came a chorus of ironic cheers when he finally made it.

'So,' said a voice from an empty armchair. 'Out walking on a day like today, eh? Any particular reason?' This was Alf the Invisible, who rarely bothered to take his reversing pills.

'I like to keep fit,' said Ronald. There was a lot of chortling at this. Wizards have a very relaxed attitude to fitness. Strolling to and from the Dining Hall is usually the extent of their exercise. And a little light stretching for another biscuit.

'Did you happen to look in the *postbox* on your way back, by any chance?' That was Fred the Flameraiser, speaking through a fog of nasty pipe smoke.

'No. Why?'

'Just wondering if your replacement Certificate has arrived.' The chortles turned into guffaws.

'No,' said Ronald shortly. 'Not yet. Any day now.'

'I *knew* he'd say that,' crowed Frank the Foreteller, slapping his thigh.

'No trouble with the *password*, I hope?' chipped in Dave the Druid – a short, plump Wizard who always wore a grubby hooded robe belted with frayed rope. He winked mischievously at his fellow Wizards, who rocked with glee.

'You know there was,' said Ronald bitterly. 'You waited until I went out, then changed it. Making me look silly in front of Brenda.'

'You look silly in front of everybody, lad,' said Frank.

'Well, I don't think it's funny,' snapped Ronald. 'What's the new one, anyway?'

'*I'm a Sorcerer, Let Me Into Here.* Move back from the fire, boy, you're steaming the place out.'

'What'sh happening?' enquired a reedy little voice. It came from the throat of Harold the Hoodwinker, the oldest Wizard, who had been lying back in his armchair with his mouth open, drooling.

'It's young Ronald,' Dave the Druid told him. 'Back from a paddle in the Wood.'

'Boy'sh a fool,' said Harold.

'Anyone care for a chocolate?' enquired Alf the Invisible. There came an eager chorus of assent. A box of chocolates rose from the table next to the empty armchair and floated around, politely offering itself to each Wizard in turn. When the box reached Ronald, all that was left was the cabbage cream that nobody ever wanted.

'Never mind, lad,' said a hawk-nosed Wizard with a long white beard and half glasses. His name was Gerald the Just, and he liked to think of himself as fair-minded. 'We're only teasing. Just our little bit of fun.'

'Yes,' said Ronald sulkily. 'At my expense.'

'True,' said Gerald. 'I'll give you that.'

It *was* true too. There were seven Wizards in the Club, but only six chairs in the Lounge – i.e., none for Ronald. He had been given one for Christmas once, but it had been 'accidentally' thrown away when the decorations came down. There was no peg for him in the Cloakroom either, and no locker for his sandwiches. He had the smallest, coldest bedroom in the highest tower, at the top of a million steps. It was all terribly unfair.

'How's your Witch aunty, young Ronald?' asked Frank, chomping on a delicious strawberry cream. 'Still sending you the home-made pimple creams, is she?'

'Don't seem to do the trick,' remarked Fred the Flameraiser, puffing away.

'He should ask her for a beard-growing potion,' chipped in Dave the Druid.

'True,' rumbled the Wizards, happily stroking their own glorious beards. 'He should.'

It was all too much. First the rain, then the password, then the mocking of the feet, then the Certificate, then the cabbage chocolate, then the Witch-for-an-aunty stuff and now they were playing the no-beard card. Ronald had had more than enough.

'Excuse me,' he snarled. 'I think I'll just go to my room. I have important things to do.'

'I *knew* he'd say that!' crowed Frank the Foreteller.

Ronald flounced out, to an uproar of guffaws and delighted knee-slapping.

## Chapter Three

# Ronald's Room

Panting heavily on account of the million steps, Ronald pushed open the door of his turret room, walked in, kicked the door closed, chucked his soggy Hat into a corner and threw himself on his disgusting tip of a bed. He hiked the hard pillow up behind his head and stared miserably around.

Nothing had changed in his absence. The room was still freezing cold and smelled funny. The old poster of Lulu Lamarre (the famous film star) in a pink evening dress still drooped from the one pin holding it to the wall. Her red lipsticked mouth smiled at him crookedly from its upside down position. Ronald didn't care. He was bored with her now.

Yep. Everything was the same. The window was

still stuck. The floorboards were still bare. The shelf on the wall was still wonky. Everything on it slid to one end. The washbasin was still cracked and the water wouldn't drain. Every time he cleaned his teeth, it took three days to empty. The wardrobe door still swung on a single hinge. The desk still wobbled. There was still no chair. If he tried lighting a fire, the chimney would still smoke.

Propped on the wobbly desk was a postcard. He knew what it said.

*I trust you received the ten pound note I sent for your birthday? On no account fritter it away. It is to be used to purchase the replacement Certificate that we are all so eager to see. Kindly write by return. Aunt Sharkadder.*

There were no kisses.

Ronald sighed. Something else he hadn't done. He hadn't written a thank you letter. But he couldn't face it now. Not yet. He was too cold, too damp, too fed up. The walk had been a washout, his Cloak and shoes were in enemy hands, he'd missed breakfast and everyone and everything had been disrespectful. The only good thing in life was the tenner in his piggy bank. Although he owed most of that to the Catalogue.

He reached under his pillow for the biscuits he kept there, then remembered he'd eaten them.

He wished that something good would happen to cheer him up. He could look at his old car magazines, he supposed. There were stacks of them in dusty piles under his bed. Or he could draw a moustache on Lulu. Or squeeze a pimple. Or get out the ten pound note and look at it again. His piggy bank lived at one end of the sloping shelf, together with his hairbrush, his hair gel, a pile of threatening letters from the Catalogue, his interesting stones collection and the copy of *My First Little Book of Wizardry*. Everything was jumbled up in a messy heap. If he tried to get at the piggy bank, the whole lot would come down.

Of course, what he should do really was get the book down and spend an hour studying. Not that it would make any difference. Magic didn't come naturally to Ronald.

The first spell in the book was *Easy Finger Sparkles*. Confidence was the thing. You had to *believe* it would work. You had to wiggle your fingers, clear your mind of doubt and say *Inky Pinky Parkle, make my fingers sparkle!* And a stream of green sparks was supposed to blaze forth, bringing gasps of astonishment and awe. The wiggling was easy, as was the rubbish rhyme. The confidence wasn't always there, though. The few sparks he managed to produce tended to sputter feebly, then die off like a cheap sparkler. He couldn't do it at all if people were watching.

He had attempted *My First Fireball* with disappointing results. Fireballs should be flaming balls of white heat with a comet tail. The rhyme went: *Bing, Bang, Bong! Fireballs are strong!* Ronald's weren't, though. They were pink and puny. They just drifted around uselessly for a bit, then popped, for some reason smelling weirdly of cheese.

He had skipped *My Little Puff of Smoke* because he was scared of setting his sleeves on fire. He had glanced at *Rabbit in a Hat!* and *See My Sleeve Doves!* and decided to leave them for another time. His skills were very limited.

There came a knock at the door. This was unusual. The thing about having the turret room was that he rarely received visitors. The Wizards couldn't be bothered with all those stairs, especially as there was only Ronald at the top of them. Even the staff conveniently forgot about him. His room never got dusted or swept. His sheets only got changed when somebody remembered, which was about twice a year.

'Yes?' he called. 'Who is it?'

'Me,' came the brisk reply. 'Open up.'

Ronald scrambled up from the bed. It was that

Crabbit girl. He recognised her voice. Come to apologise for her earlier behaviour, probably. Pushing ahead like that. It just wasn't on.

He grabbed his Hat from the corner, crammed it on his head and snatched open the door.

'Yes?' said Ronald haughtily. 'You have something to say to me?'

'Yours, I believe,' said Hattie Crabbit. She was dressed in workmanlike overalls and had replaced her basket with a toolbox. From behind her back she produced the dreaded umbrella. It had come back to haunt him.

'Well – yes. I didn't actually *choose* it, of course, it was a pres—'

'That's not the point. The point is, you dropped it in the corridor.'

'So? It's broken.'

'Put it in the bin, then.'

'I *beg* your pardon?' Ronald was shocked. Wizards didn't pick up after themselves. That was what servants were for.

'I suppose you think that's what servants are for,' said Hattie Crabbit. 'Well, I've got better things to do.'

'Really?' sneered Ronald. 'Is that so? Like what?'

'Like oiling the front door. Unclogging the

fountain. Lagging the boiler. Re-grouting the tiles in the downstairs lav. All the stuff Uncle Rube's let slide since his knee flared up.'

Ronald thought about Old Ruben Crabbit, the Clubhouse caretaker. The man was no more than a walking – no, a *crawling* list of medical ailments. The Lounge clock had behind it an entire sheaf of so-called doctor's sick notes, clearly forged. Over the past year alone, he had suffered from Spivvits, Tetters, Clover Foot, Percy's Fever, a Sprained Eye, Buzzing in the Ears, a Bad Back, Ingrowing Hairs and Recurring Knee Trouble. He spent all his time lying on the sofa watching Goblin football on spello. The only reason he hadn't been fired was that Mrs Swipe was said to be sweet on him. *Nobody* dared upset Mrs Swipe.

'Aha,' said Ronald. 'The old knee again. *I* see.'

'Yep. He's got to rest it. Doctor's orders.'

'Would that be the doctor who scribbles his sick notes on the back of old envelopes? Whose handwriting so mysteriously resembles your uncle's?'

'That's the one,' said Hattie shortly. He had clearly hit a nerve. He wondered whether to continue in the same vein, but decided not to. After all, nobody chose their relatives. He should know. He had a Witch for an aunty.

'So you're here to do Old Crabbit's job for him, are you?' he asked.

'Just helping out till he's back on his feet.'

'He's never on his feet, except to deliver sick notes.'

'Whatever. He's giving me a shilling a week.'

'A shilling?' Ronald was startled. 'Is that all?' He knew for a fact that Old Crabbit earned ten times that amount.

'Every little helps,' said Hattie. 'I'm saving up. Anyway, while I'm here, is there anything that needs fixing in your room?'

'Eh?' Ronald could hardly believe his ears. Was somebody actually offering to *fix stuff in his room*? This was a first.

'I've just carried this toolbox up a million stairs,' said Hattie. 'I might as well, while I'm here.'

'Well,' said Ronald, 'now you come to mention it, there are one or two things. The window's stuck. And the wardrobe door's missing a hinge and the sink won't empty and the desk's a bit wonky and for some reason the chimney –'

'All right,' said Hattie. 'Mind out, I'm coming in. Here, take this.' She thrust the umbrella at him, strode in and stood staring around, frowning and sniffing.

Ronald saw her eyes run over his hideous bed and felt embarrassed. Then he remembered that he was a Wizard and answered to nobody. He considered tossing the umbrella aside in a gesture of defiance, then decided not to. Not if she was going to *fix* stuff.

Hattie sighed, put the toolbox down, unclipped the lid and fished around, coming up with a chisel and a large hammer.

'Right. Window first, get some air in.' She marched to the window, angled the chisel and gave a brisk tap. Instantly, the window flew open in a shower of raindrops. 'That's better. OK, wardrobe next. I've got a hinge somewhere.'

Ronald walked to the window and stuck his head out. The rain had stopped. Well, it would, now he was back indoors.

'So how d'you get to be a Wizard, then?' asked Hattie. She was on her knees before the toolbox, sorting through a jar of screws. 'Do you need a Certificate or something?'

'Um – yes,' said Ronald.

'Can I see it?'

'No. I can't lay my hands on it right now.'

'You should have it framed. I would. I see you've got a spell book on the shelf.' She pointed at *My First Little Book of Wizardry*. 'Can you do all of them?'

'Of course,' lied Ronald. 'That's easy stuff.'

'Which one are you best at?'

'Finger Sparkles.'

'What do they do?'

'They're a sort of warning. They show you've got Magic at your fingertips. People think twice before approaching.'

'I'm not surprised. I'd run a mile from someone with fizzing fingers.'

'Yes,' said Ronald. 'They are rather effective.' Well, *his* weren't, but she didn't have to know.

'It must be fun, doing spells all the time.'

'We don't do them all the time. Except on Mervyn Day.'

'What's Mervyn Day?'

'It's the day when we remember our Club founder. You know those gold statues all over the place? The one in the lobby and the one in the Dining Hall and the one on the landing? That's him. Mervyn the Mighty.'

'So what do you do on his day?'

'Traditionally, we feast from morning to night on fish and chips. And play tricks on each other. All the statues get repainted and we sing a special song. I think it's coming up soon.'

'What do you do the rest of the time? When it's not Mervyn Day?'

'Sit around eating, mostly. Watch spello. And – er – well, go for long walks. I do, anyway.'

'Is that all?'

'I order stuff from the Catalogue.'

'Why not just conjure it up by Magic?'

'Look,' said Ronald. 'You don't understand. It's not as easy as that.'

'I bet it is. Go on, don't be shy. Show us your Finger Sparkles.'

'No,' said Ronald firmly. 'No Magic in the bedrooms.' He pointed up at the small, blinking red eye set in the ceiling. 'See?'

For safety reasons, all the Clubhouse bedrooms were fitted with Magic alarms. There had been too many fires, too many floods, too many Demons running amok in the corridors. The rule was that all major experiments must take place in the basement laboratory, although a little light, harmless conjuring was permitted in public areas. Anyone caught disobeying had to pay a penny to the Wizards' Benevolent Fund and was banned from eating between meals, which was far too high a price to pay.

'I can switch it off,' offered Hattie. 'Two seconds with a screwdriver.'

'No. I'm not in the mood.'

Hattie gave a shrug. 'Oh, well. If you can't be bothered.'

Ronald said nothing and continued to stare out of the window.

'See anything interesting?' asked Hattie after a bit.

'Not much. Mountains. A couple of goats. Sheep. An old man with a dog.'

'What sort of dog?'

'I don't know. Just a dog. Who cares?'

'I do,' said Hattie. She was standing at the wardrobe, armed with a screwdriver and a new hinge. 'I like animals.'

'You do? Why?'

Ronald had never been much of an animal lover. Aunt Sharkadder had a cat who, over the years, had regularly savaged him. Her Witch cronies owned a variety of horrible pets they referred to as their 'Familiars'. Her best friend had a cocky little hamster called Hugo. None of them liked Ronald and the feeling was mutual.

'Well, they're fun, aren't they?' said Hattie. 'And good company, if you treat them well. You can teach them tricks. Everyone should have a pet. They stop you being lonely.'

'Who says I'm lonely?' snapped Ronald. 'I've got plenty of friends. Loads. More than you, probably.'

'Calm down. I'm just saying.'

'Anyway,' said Ronald sulkily, 'anyway, there's a No Pets rule.'

'Why?'

'Because there'd be chaos. We Wizards don't do things by halves.'

This was true. Wizards are notoriously competitive and would never be content with something straightforward, like a goldfish. They would go in for unconventional pets, like gold-plated rhinos, sequinned aardvarks or flashing tigers. You wouldn't want *them* running around pooping everywhere.

A little silence fell. Ronald perched on the window sill and watched her fix the hinge.

'Do *you* have a pet, then?' he enquired after a bit. It wouldn't hurt to keep on her good side, as she was fixing stuff.

'Loads. I've got a proper menagerie at home. Three cats, two dogs, a parrot, a monkey, a donkey and a zebra called Spot. People just dump them. I'm going to open a proper shelter as soon as I've saved up. For poor, abandoned creatures that nobody wants.'

'Will it take in smelly evil ones that shouldn't be allowed to wander free?' asked Ronald. 'Because I've got a few suggestions, starting with Dudley.'

'Who?'

'Dead Eye Dudley, my aunty's cat. She got him off a pirate.'

'Well, I'm sure your aunty loves him,' said Hattie, testing the wardrobe door, which swung to and fro beautifully. 'Is that postcard from her? Ordering you to spend your birthday money on a Certificate?'

'The first one got lost in the post!' lied Ronald, adding, 'And you shouldn't read other people's correspondence.'

'I know. I did, though. Nosy, that's me. So am I right? Does she love him?'

'She does.' Ronald gave a sigh. 'She lets him stand on the table with his paw in the butter dish, licking the cream off the trifle. It's very off-putting. What are you doing now?'

'Looking for a saw. I'll trim a bit off three of your desk legs, to stop it wobbling. Then I'll unblock your chimney. That'll make a mess. Perhaps you'd like to go somewhere else for a bit?'

Rather to his own surprise, Ronald wasn't too pleased at this suggestion. He was quite enjoying himself, having a pleasant little chat while somebody else sorted his room out. She was a brisk sort of person, was Hattie Crabbit, but she certainly knew her way around a toolbox.

'It's all right,' he said. 'I'll wait.'

'I'd rather you didn't. I'll be quicker on my own.'

'I haven't got any shoes on. Mrs Swipe's got them.'

'Put on your slippers, then.'

'I can't find them,' lied Ronald. His slippers were another of Aunt Sharkadder's presents that he preferred to keep hidden.

'They're in here.' Hattie opened the wardrobe. 'Yellow chickens with pompoms, right? I saw them. Put them on.'

'I'd rather not.'

'Don't be daft. Put them on.' Hattie held out the slippers.

Reluctantly, Ronald put them on. He caught a glimpse of himself in the wardrobe mirror. He looked ridiculous, with chicken slippers and a kitten umbrella. Not a bit like a Wizard should look. But at least his feet were warm.

'Right,' said Hattie. 'Give me an hour or so. Go and do something.'

'Like what?'

'I don't know. Something interesting. You're the Wizard. And while you're gone, put that umbrella in the bin.'

She gave him a firm push, and before he knew it he was standing at the top of the steps with the door closed behind him.

The problem was, where to go? The Lounge was out of the question. He certainly wouldn't be welcome in the Dining Hall, where the servants would be laying the table for lunch. He didn't fancy the Laboratory, which was miles underground and would be locked anyway. Old Crabbit had the only key, and doubtless would be in his room on knee rest.

There was only one place he could go.

Chapter Four

# The Library

In all his time at the Wizards' Clubhouse, Ronald had never visited the Library. Studying wasn't his thing. The missing Certificate proved that.

To get really good at Wizardly Magic, you have to spend endless hours trawling through boring old spell books which send you to sleep before you've read the title. Sometimes, they fly at you in a rage and clip you round the ear. Magical books don't have much patience with slow readers.

You're supposed to take notes. You're expected to learn long incantations and copy down recipes with impossible ingredients, like badger spit and guava fruit. You have to learn to speak the language of Demons, which gives you a sore throat. You're required to read inspiring tales about Mervyn the Mighty and pit your own sorry efforts against his genius.

Then there is the practical side. This mainly involves conjuring up stuff – Fireballs, rabbits, Demons, Genies and endless flapping doves. To get this good takes months of serious experimentation in a laboratory, blowing your own eyebrows off.

Lastly, Wizardly Magic requires warm underwear. Wizards are required to stand around on mountains a lot, waving their Mystic Staffs and thundering through their beards.

Ronald wasn't a big reader and had never even seen the Laboratory. He had no spells at his fingertips, apart from the hit and miss Sparkles and the ineffectual Fireballs. Beardy thundering on mountains was a non-starter, as he hadn't got a beard and had a voice that could best be described as reedy. He had no socks, let alone warm underwear. His Wizarding consisted mostly of walking around dressed like one.

Still. Right now, the Library was the best option. Maybe there would be some books that *weren't* about Magic. Books about film stars, or cars. Maybe there would be the latest edition of the Catalogue. He could use Aunt Sharkadder's tenner and order some new slippers. Wizardly ones, with trendy curled toes

that didn't make him look like Little Miss Muffet. Although he'd have to cough up for the Cloak first.

He pushed open the door. It was dim inside. So dark, you couldn't tell the size of the room beyond. Somehow, though, you knew it was *big*. Endless racks of books stretched away into the distance and up, up into the shadows.

And it was silent. Oh, so silent. The Library was waiting for him.

Ronald took a single step forward. Even though he was wearing slippers, it echoed.

A sharp voice rapped, 'Halt!'

A motionless figure sat at a desk in a shadowy corner. This was Miss Stickler, the librarian. She wore a grey cardigan, buttoned to the throat. Her grey hair was scraped back into a severe bun. Her glasses had slanting steel frames that gave her an insectoid look. If stick insects were librarians, they would look like Miss Stickler.

This was the first time Ronald had met Miss Stickler. She took all her meals in the Library. Rumour had it that she slept there, clinging motionless to a high shelf with her long, twiggy arms.

'Ah,' said Ronald. 'Good morning, Miss Stickler.'

'No umbrellas in here. This is a Library.'

'Oh – er – sorry. Where shall I . . . ?

'The bin.' Miss Stickler waved at the bin standing prominently by the door.

Ronald dropped in the dead umbrella with a sense of relief. There. Finally he was rid of it. He would tell Aunt Sharkadder that somebody had stolen it.

'I hope you've wiped your feet,' said Miss Stickler, staring at his chicken slippers.

'Yes,' said Ronald, blushing a bit. 'I have.'

'Is there something specific you wish to peruse?'

'No,' said Ronald. 'I've just come in to – have a bit of a browse, you know? I don't suppose you have the latest issue of the Catalogue by any chance?'

Miss Stickler winced. 'This is a Library.'

'Oh. Yes, of course. Silly question.'

'Certificate?'

'What?'

'I need your Wizard's Certificate for identification.'

'Oh. Oh, I see. No, it got lost in the post. I'm waiting for a replacement.'

Miss Stickler sighed, jerked open a drawer and removed a sheet of paper from a file.

'Name?'

'Ronald the Magnificent. I'll probably be at the bottom. Last to join. But not *least*, ha, ha.'

'Hmm.' Miss Stickler didn't smile. 'Well, you don't appear to be here.'

'No? How odd.'

'Odd,' said Miss Stickler, 'but true.'

'Look,' said Ronald, 'I am a Club Member, honestly. Ask anyone. I'll bring in the Certificate the minute it arrives. Please?'

Miss Stickler gave a sigh and picked up a pen. 'Very well. Far be it for me to discourage a seeker after knowledge. But I shall make a note to that effect. You may look, but you may not borrow. Move quietly around the aisles if you please. We need to respect the other users.'

Ronald stared around the deserted library.

'Right,' he said. 'Thanks.'

'Sssssssh!' said Miss Stickler.

Hastily, he padded off down the first aisle, slippers weirdly echoing.

Instantly, there came a stirring from the books. Being Magical, they whispered to each other in rustling little voices. '*Look out . . . Here comes one . . . Straighten your spine . . . He's coming . . . He's coming!*' Some of the more excitable ones jiggled up and down, flapping their pages and squealing. '*Me! Me! Pick me!*'

The biggest, oldest, most dangerous tomes were high on the top shelves. They were chained with padlocks and plastered with yellow Post-its saying *Mind*

*Your Fingers!* and *The Library Accepts No Responsibility For Accidents.*

The papery whispering increased as Ronald hurried by. Overhead, the big dangerous books were straining forward, rattling their padlocks. One of them launched itself at his head in a wild kamikaze plunge, but was brought up short by its chain. It hung there, lashing its pages and growling. Hastily, Ronald moved on.

'*Here he comes,*' hissed a thousand ghostly voices. '*Here he comes – it's about time . . . Hey, pssst, read me, read me . . . Oi, you idiot, I'm here you know, talk about dumb . . . Hey, what's the matter with you – too difficult, am I? Well more fool you . . . Let me at him, let me at him, grrrrrr . . .*'

It was quite spooky. Ronald cleared his throat nervously. The sound was magnified a hundred times.

'Sssssssh!' came the hiss from the desk.

'Don't tell me, tell *them,*' said Ronald.

'You shouldn't be walking down that aisle,' Miss Stickler told him. 'That's for Senior Wizards. Those are specialist books, very highly strung. Try the Beginners' Section. Third aisle along on your left.'

Swallowing his pride, Ronald hastened from the scary aisle and made for the Beginners' Section. This turned out to be a low bookcase set slightly apart.

Next to it was a comfy-looking green cushion in the shape of a frog.

He crouched down and ran his eyes along the spines. *Fun with Magic. Wee Wizard Willie Goes Shopping. Poisonous Potions for Beginners. Bedtime Sleepy Spells.* The titles weren't that promising, but at least the books were quiet. Ronald flopped down on the frog cushion and folded his legs. It emitted a loud, rude noise that could have been a croak but actually wasn't.

'*Sssssshhh!*' came another sharp hiss from the faraway desk.

'Sorry!' called Ronald. 'Not me, the cushion!'

He reached out and selected a book at random. *Make Your Own Paper Wand.* Hmm. No good, he didn't have any paper. It would be rubbish anyway, he wasn't good with his hands. He put the book back. The one next to it fell out on the floor. He picked it up and examined it. *Baby's Book of Pets.*

At least it wasn't about Magic. It had pictures too, and not much writing. What was it that Hattie Crabbit had said? Something about pets being fun. *Were* they? Were they *really?* Of course, there wasn't much point in thinking about it, with the No Pets rule. Still. No harm in looking.

Ronald turned to the first page. It said, *See Whuffy the dog. Bow-wow.*

He looked at the picture of Whuffy. It looked eager and friendly, with a waggy tail. Would he choose a dog for a pet? Dogs were loyal, quite intelligent. You could teach them tricks. But of course, not all of them were like that. Some dogs were big and fierce.

Ronald quite fancied the idea of a big, fierce dog. He could train it to bite the other Wizards; that'd be good. He would call it Bruiser. It would only come to him. He would take it for walkies. He would let it off its lead and throw a ball for it and then – and then – well, then, knowing his luck, it would probably run off and pick a fight with the old man's dog he'd seen through the window. There would be vet bills. And of course, he would have to buy dog food . . . and put up with hairs everywhere . . .

Hmmm. Perhaps not a dog, then.

He turned to the next page, where there was a picture of a fluffy ginger kitten and the words, *See Tibby the kitten. Purr, purr.*

Ronald shuddered. Sweet little kittens had a habit of growing into matted furballs of malice like Dudley. Cats were out. Hastily, he turned the page.

*See Flopsy the rabbit. Hop, hop.*

Flopsy stared stupidly from the page with big, dim eyes. Ronald sneered. As far as Wizards are concerned, rabbits are props, always wanting lettuce and scrabbling like mad things whenever you pick them up. Poor pet material. Move on.

It was a very short book. There were only three more pets: a goldfish called Goldie (*bubble, bubble*), a mouse called Mary *(squeak, squeak)* and . . .

Oh. What was this? A Dragon.

There it was, on the very last page. What was a Dragon doing in a baby's pet book? It was hardly an obvious choice. On the other hand – well, why not? The pets had been very predictable so far. Clearly, the most interesting had been saved for last. Well, well. A pet Dragon. It was certainly different.

Ronald examined the picture. The Dragon was small and rather cute. It had bright green scales, round blue eyes, stubby little wings and a chubby tail with a barb on the end. Jolly red sparks were coming from its smiling mouth. There was a charming gap between its two front teeth. Below were the words:

*See Diddums the Dragon. Pthhhhhttt!*

'*Pthhhhhttt,*' muttered Ronald experimentally, trying to make the noise he thought little Diddums might make.

'Last warning!' came Miss Stickler's shrill voice.

'Sorry!' called Ronald. 'Won't happen again.'

Ronald didn't know much about Dragons. There was a Dragon called Arthur who lived with his mother in a neat bungalow somewhere down in Witchway Wood. He played the piano in a band called *The Witchway Rhythm Boys* and was certainly nobody's pet. Ronald had never seen him fly either, and he only breathed fire when he got carried away with the music. People said he was from the valleys.

Was Diddums from the valleys, or was he a different breed? Did Dragons come in different breeds? Could you send one flying out to fetch the morning paper? Would they need exercising? Did they sort their own meals out, or would you need to buy special Dragon Food in cans? He hadn't a clue. Funnily enough, he found that he was quite interested. Perhaps he should find out more.

Ronald approached the desk, where Miss Stickler was writing in a notebook.

'Um – excuse me?'

'Yes?' The insect eyes flicked up.

'Do you have anything on Dragons?'

'Of course. This is a Library.'

'Oh. Right, great. Could you point me to . . . ?'

'Dragons?'

'Yes.'

'Wait there,' commanded Miss Stickler. 'I don't want you disturbing the books again.'

She rose to her considerable height and stalked

off. Ronald edged around the desk and leaned over to see what she had been writing in her notebook.

*Run security check on spotty youth with chicken slippers. Calls himself Ronald.*

Beneath the terse line was a fanciful doodle that looked like twigs.

*WHAAAACK!*

A huge, leather bound book landed centimetres from his nose. It was massively thick and smelled faintly of brimstone.

'*The Encyclopedia of Dragonology*,' said Miss Stickler. 'Everything you need to know.'

'Oh – right. Thanks.' Ronald stared at the book in alarm. 'I don't think I – er – have time to read all of it.'

'One can always make time to read,' said Miss Stickler.

'But it'd take *weeks* to wade through that.' Ronald felt the beginnings of panic. 'Look, I'm really not that bothered. It was just an idle enquiry.'

'That is your trouble, young man,' said Miss Stickler sharply. 'You are idle. You need to develop an enquiring mind. There's a wonderful world out there. If you know nothing else, you should learn how to use an encyclopedia. You don't have to read it from cover to cover. You just dip into it and extract the information you need. Then you take notes.'

'But –'

'I shall provide you with writing materials and give you any help you require.'

'But –'

'Enough!' Miss Stickler held up a hand. 'No arguments. This is a Library.' She loomed over him, reached down and opened the cover with her twiggy fingers. 'So, young man. Let us learn about Dragons.'

Chapter Five

# Old Crabbit

It was much, much later and the Clubhouse was settling down for the night. All meals were over, the Wizards had retired and the staff were finally off duty. The Magical torches lining the long corridors burned with a spooky violet glow.

Old Crabbit was resting his knee in his room, which was next to the Kitchen. This was convenient, as he could shout through the wall for a tray or get his hot-water bottle refilled without having to lift a finger.

Right now, he was flat out on the sofa, dunking biscuits into a mug of tea and watching Goblin football on spellovision. The Rangers were playing the Wanderers. Like all Goblin matches, it was an outrageous free-for-all, with much flailing of fists, much vigorous pushing, much falling down of shorts and only an occasional fleeting glimpse of the ball. Old Crabbit thought it was a right laugh. He could have done without a visit from a Wizard in chicken slippers at this time of night. But that's what he got.

'I need to go to the Laboratory!' demanded Ronald urgently. He stood in the doorway with a sheaf of papers in his hand, covered with his own scrawled writing. His face was pale and his body drooped with exhaustion, but a fire blazed in his eyes.

'What – now?' said Old Crabbit. His eyes never left the screen.

'Yes.'

'*Right* now?'

'Right now, yes.'

'I dunno about that,' said Old Crabbit. 'Not with my knee. There's a hundred stairs down to that lab. *Get 'im, my son!*' The shout was directed at the spello. A Ranger was chasing after a Wanderer, attempting to lasso him with a football scarf. In the background, a goalkeeper could be seen slumped against his goal-post, eating a sandwich.

'You don't have to take me. Give me the key and I'll go by myself.'

'You won't be able to open the padlock. There's a knack.' Old Crabbit took a leisurely slurp of tea.

'I'll do it, all right? Just hand over the key.' Ronald was getting annoyed now.

'Hey, hey, no need to take that tone. I'm a sick man. *That's right, whack 'im!*' On the spello, the referee and a linesman were taking turns to whack each other's head with a small tree branch.

'I'm not taking a *tone*. I'm asking very reasonably for the Laboratory key. You're the caretaker, right? So take care.'

'It's *you* wants to take care,' said Old Crabbit darkly. 'I wouldn't go in that lab if I was you. Lots of activity last time I went down.'

'When was that?'

Old Crabbit looked shifty. 'Don't remember. Bin a while, with my back.'

'I thought it was your knee?'

'It's both. Back *and* knee.'

'What sort of activity?'

'Well, the rabbits have been breedin',' reflected Old Crabbit. 'So have the doves. And there's a nasty little Demon runnin' around. Broke out of his bottle. Went for me ankle; still got the scar. Stuffed crocodile's come down off the rafter, crawled off again, dunno where to. Then there's the gorilla.'

'*Gorilla?*'

'Well, I think it's a gorilla. Looks like one. 'Cept for the spaniel ears and the gills. He comes and he goes. Name's Reg. You lot never clear up after yourselves. Think it's beneath you. Place is crawlin' with yer experimental leftovers.' Old Craddock gave a sniff. 'Well, *I* can't do it, not now. Not with my knee. *Oi! Goalie! What you playin' at!*'

A roar went up from the spello. The Rangers' centre forward was lying in his own goal, curled up in the mud and refusing to let go of the ball. The goalie was still leaning against the post, licking mustard off his fingers and staring into space, unaware that his shorts had fallen down.

'I don't believe a word of it,' said Ronald. 'You're just making it up to put me off.'

'Put you off what?' came a voice. Hattie Crabbit was standing right behind him, toolbox in hand.

'Going down to the lab,' said Ronald. 'I need the key, but your uncle's not being very helpful.'

'He won't 'ave the knack,' said Old Crabbit.

'So you keep saying,' snapped Ronald. 'But you're forgetting that I can open it by Magic if necessary.'

'Don't need the key, then, do you?' said Old Crabbit.

'You can do that, can you?' asked Hattie. 'Open things with Magic?'

'Of course,' lied Ronald. 'Child's play.'

'It's just that in the kitchen, they say . . .' She trailed off.

'What? What do they say?'

'Nothing.'

'No, go on. What do they say?'

'Well . . . that you're a bit rubbish at the whole Magic thing. Sorry. It's just what I heard.'

'Nonsense,' said Ronald tightly. 'Of course I can open things. A simple Fireball should do it.'

This wasn't true, of course. Using the key would be so much better.

'How come your bedroom window was stuck, then?' asked Hattie.

'I told you. We're not allowed to use Magic in the bedrooms.'

'Take more than a Fireball to shift that padlock,' said Old Crabbit from the sofa. 'I'm tellin' you now. You needs the key. An' the knack.'

'Look!' said Ronald, really annoyed now. 'Look, Crabbit, I am a *Wizard*. That means I employ you. As your employer, I insist that you take me down to the Laboratory now, this instant!'

'I'll take you if you like,' offered Hattie. 'I've got the caretaker's knack, it's in the blood. And I can see you're all fired up about something.' She reached past him and took a key from a row of hooks on the wall. 'Come on, let's go.'

The torches flared up helpfully as they walked along the corridor. Hattie strode in front with Ronald shuffling along behind in his chicken slippers. It was very annoying, how she always led the way. He was a Wizard. Wizards were supposed to go first. On the other hand, he didn't actually know where the Laboratory was.

'So what will you do down in the lab?' enquired Hattie over her shoulder. 'Practise your Finger Sparkles?'

'No. Something rather more ambitious than that.'

'Is it a secret?'

'Well – yes.'

'You can tell me. Go on. What?'

Ronald debated. He was about do something against the rules. On the other hand, he would quite like to impress her, after what they'd said about him in the kitchen.

'Oh, you know,' he said casually. 'Just a little matter of Summoning a Dragon.'

Hattie stopped in her tracks. 'A *Dragon*?'

'Yes.'

'Hot, swoopy thing with scales?'

'Yes. I've copied the spell down. Surprisingly straightforward, actually. Basic ingredients. There's a store cupboard down there, apparently. Should have everything I need.'

'Why a Dragon?'

'Why not? You told me to go and do something interesting and I did. I went to the Library and swotted up on Dragons. And now I'm going to summon one. You said yourself that everyone should have a pet.'

'I meant a goldfish or something.'

'Too boring. A Dragon's much more suitable for a Wizard. I'm thinking of calling it – um – Diddums.'

'*Diddums?*'

'Yes.'

'Diddums. Right. I see. Hmm. Well, I don't know much about Dragons.' Hattie began walking down the corridor again, boots echoing.

'I do, though,' said Ronald. He caught her up and waved his notes in her face. 'In fact, I'm a bit of an expert. I read an entire encyclopedia. Ask me a question. Go on.'

'What do they eat?'

'Firewood!' cried Ronald excitedly. 'They forage for themselves, so they're cheap to feed. Ask me another one.'

'What about exercise?'

'No problem. They take themselves off for flights. You can train them to fetch the newspaper at the same time. Do another one.'

'What about the whole fire-breathing thing?'

'You can teach them to control it. But it's a really useful feature, isn't it? Just think. No need for matches. Toast on demand. And they're really good at guarding treasure, so my money will be safe.'

'I don't want to put a damper on things,' said Hattie, 'but what about the No Pets rule?'

'Well, Hattie,' said Ronald. 'It so happens that I'm a bit of a rule-breaker.' He rather liked the way that sounded. It made him sound a bit reckless. A bit daring. The sort of guy who swaggers around conjuring up Dragons whenever the mood takes him. 'Anyway,' he added, 'if I don't like it I can always send it back.'

'You can't do that!' cried Hattie, shocked. 'A pet's not just for – for a *summoning*. It's a living thing, with feelings. It feels pain, it feels hurt, it . . .'

'All right, no need to go on. I'll probably keep it anyway.'

'Where?'

'In my room. Nobody ever goes up there.'

'*I* went up there,' Hattie pointed out. Ronald stared at her. She wouldn't tell on him. Would she?

'Don't look so worried,' said Hattie. 'Your secret's safe with me. But it can't stay cooped up for ever. How will you let it out without anyone noticing there's a Dragon with a newspaper flying in and out of your window?'

'I'll let it out at night. It'll be fine.'

'If you say so. But personally, I don't think you've thought it through. Here we are.'

They had reached a low archway set in the wall. A flight of stone steps descended into shadow. Hattie took the nearest torch from its niche.

'I'll go first,' she said. 'Some of the steps look a bit dodgy.'

Ronald didn't argue.

## Chapter Six

# The Laboratory

The crumbling steps wound down, down, down, finally ending at a low door made of stout oak. A large padlock secured the heavy bolt.

'Right,' said Hattie. She dumped her toolbox on the bottom step. 'Hold this.' She thrust the torch at Ronald. 'Don't set your Hat on fire.'

'Will this take long, do you think?' he asked. Now he was here, he was eager to get started. Well – sort of eager. Eager and nervous at the same time.

'Well, we'll just have to see, won't we?' Hattie inserted the key into the lock. There was an instant click. 'There you go. Hooray for the caretaker's knack.' She removed the padlock. 'OK, it's all yours.'

Ronald stared at the door. Suddenly, he didn't feel quite so keen. It was all happening a bit too quickly.

'I'll leave you to it,' said Hattie. 'Keep the torch, it might be dark in there.' She bent down and hefted the toolbox.

'Where are you going?' asked Ronald.

'To bed. Why? Are you getting cold feet?'

'No,' snapped Ronald. 'Of course not. A Wizard has no fear.' But he still made no move to open the door.

'Oh, good grief,' sighed Hattie. 'What *is* it with you and doors?' She pushed past him and gave the door a short, sharp shove. It flew open with a squeal.

Beyond lay pitch blackness. Blackness out of which came rather worrying sounds. Startled little scurryings and scamperings and the soft flap of wings. There was a smell too. A gassy, chemical smell. It was the smell of stale Magic, mixed in with something else.

'Go on, then,' said Hattie.

'I'm *going*,' snapped Ronald. 'I'm just wondering what's making those weird noi— *arrrrgh!*'

He staggered backwards, flailing, as a large flock of small white birds exploded from the doorway. One collided with his Hat, knocking it off his head. Another knocked the torch out of his hand. Another pecked him on the ear before streaking off to join its comrades, who were flapping away up the stairs, shedding feathers and cooing hysterically.

Ronald stared down at his Robe of Mystery. Oh, great. Just great. Dove poop. All over his shoulders and down his front.

'Wow!' said Hattie. 'Doves gone bad. What was *that* about?'

'Revenge,' said Ronald grimly. 'All those years of being stuffed up sleeves and jumpers. Yuck, what a *mess*!'

'Here.' Hattie fished in the pocket of her overalls and pulled out an oily rag. 'Best I can do.'

Ronald dabbed ineffectually at the stains. It didn't work. He was only spreading them. He handed the rag back and cast around for his Hat, the torch and his notes, which he had dropped in the kerfuffle.

'I'm not surprised they're fed up,' said Hattie. 'That's no way to treat birds. Stuffing them up your j— oh!' She broke off and pointed. 'Look!'

A brown rabbit was squatting in the doorway. It was staring up at them, nose twitching. Hattie set down her toolbox and scooped it up. The rabbit made no protest. It just lay in her arms like a saggy old cushion.

'Put it down,' said Ronald. 'It's a stupid prop. It just wants lettuce.'

'It's sweeeet,' cooed Hattie, nuzzling the rabbit's ears. 'I like rabbits.'

'Just as well,' said Ronald. 'Because I think there might be rather a lot of them.'

In the lab, wall torches were coming on – erratically at first, but then with a steady violet glow. They shone on rafters whitened with droppings and alive with scuttling spiders. They shone on ancient benches, laid out in rows. They shone on cobwebby glass equipment and dusty test tubes and cold Bunsen burners –

But most of all, they shone on rabbits. Startled eyes. Frozen limbs. Twitching noses. There were rabbits *everywhere*. Under benches, behind pillars, in corners, everywhere. And where there are rabbits –

'*Uggh!*' said Ronald. 'What a pong. Look at that floor, it's *encrusted!*' He pulled off his Hat and waved it under his nose.

'Go in, then,' said Hattie, poking him in the back. 'Or are you scared of spiders?'

'I'm going. I'm *going*, all right? It's just that . . .'

'What?'

'It's just that your uncle mentioned that a Demon's broken out of a bottle. And there might be a gorilla. Called Reg. With spaniel ears and gills. Although I think he was lying.'

'Well, there's only one way to find out. Shall I go first?'

'No! Certainly not. Wizards go first.'

Cautiously, he stepped through the doorway. Instantly, his slippers welded themselves to the floor.

'Poor things,' said Hattie. 'They've been digging holes, look, trying to find a way out.' Gently, she put down the brown rabbit, who hopped off to join its friends. 'Whoo! It's *spooky* in here.'

It was. Yellowing charts showing the signs of the zodiac drooped from the walls. The stained benches were cluttered with dusty, long abandoned experiments. A full-size skeleton hung from a hook. It was shrouded in cobwebs and grinning like an idiot. Someone had stuck a paper party hat on its head.

Ronald peeled a slipper from the floor and attempted another step. It was like walking on congealed treacle.

'What d'you think those are for?' asked Hattie, pointing up at a rafter from which hung two rusting chains, several metres apart.

'The stuffed crocodile,' Ronald told her knowledgeably. 'There's always one in a Wizards' lab. Traditional. Not sure where it is now, though.'

Nervously, he peered around. Plenty of rabbits, but no sign of a crocodile. No spaniel-eared gorilla either, which was good news.

'*Jvark?*' shrieked a sudden voice from above, making them jump.

Glaring down at them was a small, red, scaly creature with webbed feet, two tiny horns and a forked tail. It was perched right in the middle of a rafter, little legs swinging and crimson eyes glittering in the violet light. It held a tiny pitchfork in its claw.

'What's that?' asked Hattie. 'An Imp, or something?'

'It's a Demon,' said Ronald. 'Leave this to me. Wizards' work.'

'*Jvark?*' screeched the Demon again. '*Jvark?*'

'What?' said Ronald. He couldn't speak Demon.

'*Jvark?*'

'What?'

'*Jvark?*'

'What?'

'This isn't really getting anywhere, is it?' said Hattie. 'I'd move on.'

'Look,' said Ronald to the Demon. 'I haven't a clue what you're saying. Speak English.'

'OK. Me good at languages,' said the Demon, adding rudely, 'Unlike useless vizards. Who ugly girl viz iron box?'

'Look who's talking,' said Hattie crossly. 'At least I don't come out of a jar.'

'It bottle, not jar!'

'Same difference.'

'*Not!* Stupid girl! Jar common. Bottle *classy!*'

'Well, obviously. If it's made of glass, it's glassy.'

'*Classy*, not glassy, stupid girl!'

'Well, it doesn't really matter, does it?' broke in Ronald. Things were getting out of hand. 'Pipe down, you! Less of the insults.' He had never met a Demon, but had heard the other Wizards talking. He hoped what he'd heard was right. If you're firm with them, they back down. Well, the smaller ones do. Apparently.

'That's right, Ron, you tell it,' said Hattie. 'Rude little squirt.' She set her toolbox down and began wandering around, sniffing test tubes, peering at dusty crucibles and running her finger along filthy surfaces. 'Ugh. Uncle's really let it go in here. Look at the state of that skeleton. I don't like to think of the last time *that* saw a duster.'

'*Knshvak!*' snarled the Demon overhead, waving its trident. Its tail lashed furiously and its eyes bulged.

'What?' said Ronald.

'*Knshvak!* Go *away!*'

'You're the Wizard,' said Hattie. 'Just tell it to shut up.'

'Another word and you're toast,' Ronald told the Demon. 'I mean it, mind.'

'That's it, Ron,' said Hattie. 'You told it.' She was poking around on a cluttered bench.

She picked up a large green bottle with a broken neck. 'I wonder what was in here?'

'Zat *mine*!' the Demon informed her. 'You put down!'

'I thought I told you to shut up,' snapped Ronald. He turned to Hattie. 'It's right, though. I wouldn't touch anything, if I were you. Some of this old stuff might be a bit delicate.'

'Fair enough,' said Hattie. 'Just looks like old junk to me. But you're the Wizard, Ron.'

He thought about telling her not to keep calling him Ron. But perhaps now wasn't the time. Not when she was being supportive. Besides, it would be good to have her there if the crocodile showed up. Or Reg.

'Right,' he said. 'I'd better get started. The ingredients cupboard should be somewhere.'

'Is this it?' said Hattie.

She walked over to a dark alcove. Tucked away at the back was a tall, rickety cupboard. The chalked words *Magical Ingredients! Beware!* were scrawled across the door. Below was a badly drawn skull and crossbones. Some joker had added comedy sunglasses and a bow tie.

Hattie wrenched open the door and various boxes and packets tumbled out, spilling their contents on the floor.

'Careful!' howled Ronald, starting forward, forgetting the slippers, which stayed right where they were. He clutched wildly at the dangling skeleton. The Demon smirked. The skeleton grinned, but only because it had to.

'Stop fussing,' said Hattie. 'It's only a bit of powder. The floor's a mess already. Needs a proper job doing with a shovel . . .'

'Some powders are highly dangerous! You mustn't mix them up!'

'Well, somebody's got to make a start or we'll be here all night. We need to get cracking before the gorilla arrives.'

## Chapter Seven

# The Summoning

'Have you got a list of what you need?' asked Hattie impatiently.

'Yes. Just a minute, I'll find the recipe.' Ronald shuffled through his notes. A few rabbits were cautiously venturing from their hiding places. One hopped on to his foot, and he kicked it off impatiently.

Hattie gave him a hard look, then bent down and began stroking its ears. 'There, there. Take no notice of the nasty Wizard.'

'Ah, here it is.' Ronald selected a crumpled sheet and shoved the rest of his notes on the nearest handy bench where a complicated-looking experiment was set up, taking up most of the available space. It looked more recent than the others. The glass tubing was dust free and the test tubes had some kind of blue liquid in them rather than mould. A yellow Post-it was attached to the bench. It said: *Vitally Important Experiment in Progress. Do Not Disturb. Frank the Foreteller.*

'So what do you need?' asked Hattie.

'A pound of Dried Lava,' read out Ronald, 'six ounces of Best Brimstone, a teaspoon of Sulphur, a pinch of Charcoal, half a pint of Mixed Venom and eight drops of Drago Thunderbum's Concentrated Lizard Oil. And I'll need a box of matches.'

Slippers peeling unwillingly from the floor at each step, he headed for the cupboard. The Demon sat up, clearly hoping for another accident. He ran his eyes over the shelves, which were in serious disarray. Sighing, he began rummaging around.

'*Knshvak!*' remarked the Demon under its breath. '*Shlockl tvit.*'

'That's enough from you,' said Hattie. 'You don't want to find yourself on the wrong end of his Finger Sparkles.' That seemed to do the trick. The Demon curled its lip, then subsided into sulky silence.

It took a while, but finally Ronald's arms were piled with boxes and brown paper bags, a selection of rusty spoons, a set of old-fashioned balance scales, a tiny corked vial of oil and an old milk bottle half full of evil-looking brown liquid.

He tottered back to the handy bench and dumped his haul on the surface, knocking over the Bunsen burner, which in turn knocked over the rack of test tubes. The tubes rolled everywhere, disgorging blue liquid. Two of them fell on the floor and broke. Oh, well. With a shrug, Ronald swept the remaining bits of Frank's vitally important experiment on to the floor, leaving only the burner and his own stuff.

'Ha!' he muttered. 'Bet you didn't foretell *that*.'

'Now what?' asked Hattie.

'Now I grind everything up. There's a pestle and mortar on that bench over there; would you mind?'

Hattie walked across to a bench on which was set a heavy stone bowl with a smooth stone for grinding. 'This?'

'That's it. Oh, and see if you can find a stick of chalk somewhere.'

'Why d'you need chalk?'

'To draw the Magic Circle. For the Dragon, when it arrives.'

'Chalk won't work on this floor. You can't chalk on dove poop and rabbit droppings. You'll have to carve it. There's a chisel in my toolbox, that'll do it.'

'Fine,' said Ronald. 'Thanks.'

He sat down at the bench, rolled up his sleeves and began weighing, measuring and pouring, frequently

consulting the recipe to be sure he got it exactly right. Overhead, the Demon sat on the rafter, swinging its little legs and smouldering.

'I'll do the Circle if you like,' offered Hattie, returning with the chisel, a length of string and a tape measure. 'Where d'you want it?'

'In the middle, away from the benches.'

'OK. How big?'

'Depends on how big a Dragon I want.'

'I'll do a small one. Pocket-sized.'

'Not *that* small. I don't want to step on it when I get out of bed. About the size of your toolbox, I should think. Don't interrupt me now, I'm concentrating.'

Ronald was glad she had offered, though. He had never attempted to draw a circle, Magic or otherwise. He had a feeling it was harder than it looked.

He poured the dry ingredients into the mortar, picked up the pestle and began to grind. The resulting smell was terrible. It reeked of volcanoes and dried-up acid lakes. It got up the nostrils. It made the eyes weep.

Holding his breath, Ronald added the Mixed Venom and the Lizard Oil. The mixture seethed and the smell got even worse. The Demon scurried hastily along the rafter into a far corner, well out of the way.

'I've done the Circle,' said Hattie, standing back and examining her work with a critical eye. 'Now what?'

Ronald consulted the recipe. 'Heat to boiling point. I need a glass flask. Can you see one anywhere?'

Hattie stared around, spotted a grubby-looking flask on the next bench along, picked it up and handed it to Ronald. 'This do?'

'Perfect. Oh, and find me some tongs.' There was a little silence. 'Please.'

'Honestly,' sighed Hattie. 'I'm not your *assistant*, you know.' But she set off again and returned with a pair of blackened tongs.

Ronald attempted to lift the mortar. It was much heavier than it looked.

'Shall I do that?' offered Hattie.

'No, no, I can do it.'

'Don't drop it, then.'

'He vill,' said the Demon from the corner.

'I won't. I *won't*, all right?'

Arms shaking, Ronald hefted the mortar and carefully poured the stinking sludge into the flask. He righted the burner and turned on the tap. Gas hissed. Fingers trembling, he fumbled with a match.

'Try holding it the other way up,' suggested Hattie.

'All right, I can see, I can *see*.' Ronald finally lit the

match and applied it to the gas. A blue flame shot up. Using the tongs, he gripped the flask and held it over the flame.

'Don't drop it,' said Hattie again.

'He vill,' said the Demon.

'Look, just *stop*, will you? I'm *doing* it.' Little wisps of foul-smelling smoke escaped as the mixture began to simmer.

'Poo,' said Hattie, holding her nose. 'That is *gross*. Will this take long?'

'You have to be patient with these things,' croaked Ronald. 'This is advanced Magic. Can't be rushed. Um – you couldn't hold my nose for me, could you?'

'No, I couldn't. Should it look like that, d'you think?'

The mixture in the flask was slowly turning a dark, evil-looking green. It was heaving and bubbling, giving off thick smoke that was spreading everywhere. Up on the rafter, the Demon was having a noisy choking fit. The rabbits were nowhere to be seen.

'Certainly,' said Ronald firmly, although actually he didn't have a clue because the recipe didn't say. 'Exactly the shade I'm looking for. Right, I think that's probably hot enough. Stand back.'

Holding the tongs at arm's length, he advanced upon the Circle. Carefully, he set down the smoking flask exactly in the middle.

'Now what?' asked Hattie.

'The incantation,' said Ronald.

'What's that?'

'A rhyming chant.'

'Why not say so, then?'

'Shush,' said Ronald. He was back at the bench, studying his notes. 'I have to memorise it.'

'Why not just read it out?'

'Because I need my hands free to make important Magical Gestures. Right, I think I've got it. Stand back, Hattie, this bit's dangerous.'

He put down his notes and advanced to the Circle again, slippers still gluing themselves to the floor. Impatiently, he stooped and pulled them off. Reciting an incantation was a serious business. You had to look the part. Bare feet would be better than chicken slippers. Only just, mind.

He stood with his toes just touching the Circle's edge. This was the moment. It was essential to be word-perfect. This would be a challenge. *Inky Pinky Parkle* it wasn't.

He took a deep breath – then hesitated. Beads of sweat broke out on his forehead. He clenched his fists. Could he *really* do this?

Yes. He had to. Now was the time to attempt real, grown-up Magic. Magic that went way beyond Finger

Sparkles. In front of an audience. It was a shame he wasn't wearing his Cloak of Darkness. But he could do without it, couldn't he? Confidence, that's what really mattered.

'He rubbish,' jeered the Demon. 'He can't do.'

'Yes he can,' flashed Hattie. 'Just leave him alone, will you?'

Ronald took another breath, fixed his eyes on the flask, crossed his fingers for luck and threw up his arms.

'Go, Ron!' shouted Hattie supportively. 'Show us how it's done!'

'*Come, thou beast from unknown climes!*' squawked Ronald, in his reedy voice.

> '*Hearken to a Wizard's rhymes!*
> *Hear my Summons! Come with speed!*
> *Of a Dragon I have need!*
> *Time to leave thy hidden lair!*
> *Spread thy wings! Embrace the air!*
> *No more doubts or hesitating!*
> *Noble Dragon, I am waiting!*'

The echoes died away. Ronald lowered his arms and waited.

Nothing happened. The flask just sat there, smoking.

He waited some more . . .

Still nothing.

And some more . . .

Nothing.

'See?' sneered the Demon. 'Rubbish.'

'You did it very nicely, I thought,' said Hattie, emerging from the corner. 'You didn't fluff any words. And I liked the arm waving thing. Never mind him.' She glared at the Demon.

Ronald turned his back on the Circle, where the flask still sat smoking quietly.

'Look,' he said, 'I know you're trying to help, but you don't have to say anything.'

'Maybe some of the ingredients are past their sell by date,' suggested Hattie.

'Maybe.' Ronald gave a sigh. 'But whatever the reason –'

*FLASH!* A white, blinding light!

*WHOOOOOOMPH!*

A wave of heat hit him in the back, knocking all the air from his lungs. His feet left the floor. For a terrifying, slow-motion second he was airborne – then, with a cry, he crashed heavily on to his knees, missing the skeleton by a whisker. Over in the corner, the Demon fell off the rafter. Hattie staggered back with a startled squeal and covered her eyes.

The Laboratory was filled with thick, black, stinking, billowing smoke. It was everywhere. Forget the green smoke from the flask, which was nothing compared to this. This was the mother of all smokes. This smoke was *smokin'*!

Ronald was on all fours, eyes tightly closed, choking and gasping like a traction engine. His knees were agony. His throat burned. His back hurt. He wasn't at all sure that he'd ever be able to get up.

'Ron,' came Hattie's voice in his ear. It sounded muffled. Perhaps he'd burst his eardrums.

'*Arrrgh*,' moaned Ronald. '*Owwww!* Leave me alone.' He burst into another fit of coughing.

'Get up, idiot. *Look*!'

Slowly, painfully, Ronald struggled to his feet and stood swaying, eyes still tightly closed. He felt around the back of his Robe. There was a huge hole in it. It had scorched edges.

'*Look!*' insisted Hattie. Urgently, she shook his shoulder. 'Open your eyes!'

Ronald tried to, but it hurt. His lashes seemed to have welded themselves together. He rubbed them hard. They peeled halfway open, and he squinted blearily. Then, despite the pain, he opened them wide.

The black smoke had vanished. All gone, cleared

away, just like that. The flask was nowhere to be seen. Instead . . . in the Circle . . .

*In the Circle was a Dragon!*

'You did it, Ron!' whooped Hattie, clapping him on the back. 'Oops, sorry, did that hurt? But you *did* it!'

Ronald said nothing. *He had Summoned a Dragon.* The shock had taken all words away. His brain was refusing to work properly. But he knew one thing.

He wasn't going to call it Diddums.

Chapter Eight

# The Dragon

The Dragon wasn't at all what Ronald was expecting. It bore no resemblance to little Diddums whatsoever, apart from being green. Its eyes were yellow and baleful, not round and blue. Two bony lumps with flaps on that might be ears sat atop its long, narrow head. A pair of bat-like wings was folded against its scaly sides. A frill of leathery spikes ran along its back, getting smaller along the lizard-like tail, which had a vicious-looking barb at the end. Sharp talons extended from its feet. It wasn't chubby. It was lean, mean and *angry*-looking.

It crouched on all fours, tail swishing and head moving slowly from side to side, taking in its surroundings. Its eyes moved uninterestedly past the gibbering Demon – past Hattie – and finally came to rest on Ronald.

It tensed. Its eyes became yellow slits. A low growl started up from somewhere deep in its chest. Slowly, its jaws opened, exposing a picket fence of sharp, soot-stained teeth. It took a deep, rasping breath.

*Whoooooosh!* A jet of pale green fire shot out, setting fire to Ronald's Hat.

Ronald staggered back with a small scream. He snatched off the Hat, threw it on the floor and automatically began stamping out the flames before he remembered that his feet were bare. '*Ouch! Ow, ow, ow!*'

The Dragon watched with satisfaction. It drew in another breath. And then –

'*Bad* Dragon!' scolded Hattie. She strode forward, wagging her finger. 'That is *not* acceptable behaviour.'

'Hattie!' croaked Ronald. 'Get back! Don't antagonise it!'

'Nonsense. It needs a firm hand. *Sit!*'

The Dragon looked surprised. Its eyes rolled up and stared at Hattie. Then, to everyone's amazement – it sat!

'You see?' said Hattie. She picked up one of Ronald's abandoned slippers and waved it in the

Dragon's face. 'Fire up again and it's the naughty step for you, my lad.'

The Dragon gave a small whimper and cringed.

'Woo!' gasped the Demon. 'Zat *amazink*!'

The Dragon ignored it. It was gazing anxiously up at Hattie, lizardy tail wagging feebly, clearly wanting approval. Hattie reached down and patted its scaly head. The Dragon stretched out a long green tongue and licked her hand.

'Shake a claw, then,' said Hattie. The Dragon meekly lifted a taloned foot and placed it in her waiting palm. 'There's a clever boy. Can you do any other tricks, I wonder? Roll over? Play dead?'

'Will you *look* at this!' said Ronald. He didn't want any more demonstrations. 'Look what it's done to my *Hat*!' Crossly, he picked up his still smoking hat and jammed it back on his head.

Cautiously, the Demon sidled up to the Magic Circle. It peered at the Dragon, then poked it with the blunt end of its pitchfork. The Dragon looked at it sideways in a funny way but otherwise did nothing.

'*Spluzt*,' said the Demon. 'It *tame*.' It stepped away and stared at Hattie with new respect. The Dragon continued to sit with its tongue hanging out, eyes on Hattie, awaiting further instructions.

'All right,' said Hattie. 'You can come out now. No sudden moves, mind.'

The Dragon rose to its feet, stretched out its bat wings, waddled out of the Circle, stared around – and sneezed. Green sparks sprayed from its nostrils. Guiltily, it looked up at Hattie, like a puppy who has made an accidental puddle.

'It's all right,' said Hattie. 'You can't help that.' She turned to Ronald. 'Come and have a look at it, then. It's your Dragon.'

Ronald stayed right where he was.

'Go on. Stroke it. It won't bite.'

'It'll burn, though,' said Ronald.

'No it won't. Just show it who's master.'

Reluctantly, Ronald took a step forward. Just one. The Dragon tensed. The low growling started up again.

'*Now then!*' said Hattie sharply. 'What did I just say?'

The Dragon went quiet. It was still tense, though. Its yellow eyes were showing the whites.

'Scratch it behind the ears,' suggested Hattie. 'All animals like that.'

'Not likely.' Ronald stared at the Dragon. The Dragon stared malevolently back.

Ronald said, 'I don't like it.'

'What d'you mean, you don't *like* it? You haven't even got to know it yet.'

'I don't *want* to get to know it.'

'Why not? Give it a chance. It'll get used to you.'

'It won't. It hates me.'

'Don't be silly.'

'It does. I don't want it.'

'Well,' said Hattie. 'You're stuck with it now.'

'No I'm not. I'm going to send it back to wherever it came from.'

'Go on, then,' said Hattie disgustedly. 'If you want to be really mean.'

'I will,' said Ronald. 'I *will*.'

Then he thought about this. Actually, he wouldn't. He'd love to, but he couldn't. Nowhere in the encyclopedia had he noticed anything about how to send back unwanted Dragons. He really should have thought of that. He would have to go back to the Library again. Hopefully, Miss Stickler could help him.

'I can't do it right now,' he hedged. 'I'll need different ingredients.'

'Well, there you are, then. Give it a day or two at least. It'll calm down. Tell you what. I'll empty out my toolbox and we'll take it up to your room. I'll help you get it settled in.'

'I don't want it in my room.'

'Well, what are you going to do with it, then? Leave it down here? Just shut the door and forget about it?'

'No do zat!' begged the Demon. '*Me* no vant it.'

Hattie upended her toolbox. Hammers, chisels, saws and jars of nails cascaded on to the floor.

'I'll come down and pick them up in the morning. Right. In you go, mister.' And with no more ado, she picked up the Dragon and stuffed it into the box. Its head remained sticking up, eyes glaring daggers at Ronald.

'*Down!*' instructed Hattie. The head bobbed down and she closed the lid. 'Right, that's sorted. Shall we go? Or do you want to clear up a bit? You've made a terrible mess.'

Indeed, Ronald had. Frank's vital experiment was in bits all over the floor. His own notes were a charred ruin. So were his slippers.

'No,' said Ronald. 'I don't.' Since when did Wizards clear up after themselves?

'Let's go, then.' Hattie picked up the toolbox and made for the door.

'*Vrk sputz,*' hissed the Demon. '*Gute* riddance!'

Ronald waved a fist at it, then hurried after Hattie before the door closed.

Outside, Hattie set down the toolbox, yanked the door shut, reset the padlock and pocketed the key.

'That's it. Come on, let's hurry. I'd like to get to bed some time tonight.' And she began climbing the stairs, toolbox swinging, with Ronald close behind.

Their footsteps died away. Behind the door, all was silent in the Laboratory. Then there came a noise. A new noise. It was the crawling, slithery sort of noise that a stuffed crocodile might make.

'*Knash*,' hissed the Demon. '*Zacroc!*'

The crawly slithering noise was followed by a crashing noise, accompanied by some vigorous chest-thumping. The sort of noise a spaniel-eared gorilla with gills might make.

'*Ach!*' screeched the Demon. '*Zere* you is, Reg. You miss all ze excitement!'

Ronald couldn't believe his eyes when he stepped into his room.

*It had been fixed.*

A new curtain hung over the window. It was a cheerful orange. There was a matching rug on the floor. The shelf had been straightened and all his belongings set out in a neat line, with the piggy bank standing proudly in the middle. The crack on the washbasin had been sealed with some sort of filler.

The desk legs were all the same length, and there was even an actual *chair*. It was basic, but it was a *chair*. A fire glowed in the hearth. A real fire!

Best of all, though, was his bed. Someone had *made* it. There were clean sheets. Instead of his bedspread being the usual crumpled mess, it was laid neatly on top, without a single wrinkle. No sign of Lulu's poster, he noticed. But he wasn't going to complain about that.

'Wow!' said Ronald. 'I *say*!'

'Better?' asked Hattie.

'Better? It's a miracle!'

'Oh, I wouldn't say that. I fixed what needed fixing and got the maids to sort you out clean sheets and whatnot.'

'But – it's incredible! You found me a *chair*! And you fixed the sink . . . and the curtain . . . the rug . . . I don't know what to say.'

'That's OK,' said Hattie. 'Just doing my job. Now. Let's get this little fellow out of the box.'

'Must we?'

'Certainly. The sooner he gets used to his new home the better.' Hattie dumped down the toolbox and opened the lid. 'Come on, then, mister. Out you come.'

The Dragon's head appeared over the rim. It

spotted Ronald and its ears went back. Ronald clutched at his Hat and dived out of the line of fire.

'Calm down,' said Hattie, stroking the scaly head. 'You're just a bit confused, aren't you? Look at the nice fire!'

The Dragon looked at the nice fire. Its eyes reflected the glowing coals. It seemed to be relaxing under Hattie's soothing hand.

'It doesn't want to come out,' said Ronald.

'He will when he's ready. He's getting his bearings. Listen. He's purring.' A low, contented rumbling was indeed coming from the Dragon's chest. It seemed transfixed by the fire. 'What are you going to call him? I'm guessing not Diddums.'

'No,' said Ronald. 'It's definitely not a Diddums. And how do you know it's a him? It might be a her.'

'He's a boy,' said Hattie firmly. 'You can tell. He needs a boy's name. What about Flame? Flambo? Scorchy?'

'No.' Ronald remembered the jet of flame that had nearly demolished his hat. 'Nothing fiery. I don't want to encourage it. *Him*, I mean.'

The Dragon gave a yawn, exposing his throat. It was like looking down a mine shaft with a lot of sharp, black, jagged rocks around the entrance. He rested his chin on the edge of the box. Firelight danced in his eyes.

'What, then?'

'I suppose it should begin with a D,' said Ronald.

'Why?'

'Well, it rolls off the tongue, doesn't it? Think of D names. What about Denis?'

'Hmm. Denis the Dragon. I'm not sure it's quite right.'

'Darren? Dirk? Desmond?'

'Mmm – no.'

'Derek?'

'No. What about Donald? It might help you to bond if your names rhyme.'

'It won't,' said Ronald. 'Keep going. Dean? Douglas? Dave, Denzil, Dermot . . .'

'Wait! Go back one.'

'What – Denzil?'

'That's good. I've got a cousin called Denzil.'

'What's he like?'

'Horrible. He picks his nose and wipes it on his jumper. He's got dreadful habits.'

'Right,' said Ronald. 'That'll do. Denzil it is.'

'Good. Well, I'm off. I'll leave the box and pick it up tomorrow.'

'Wait a minute!' Ronald was horrified. 'I thought

you said you'd help me settle it in. *Him*, I mean.'

'He *is* settled in,' said Hattie. 'Look at him. He's dropping off.' Indeed, the newly named Denzil's eyelids were drooping.

'I don't trust it. Him.'

'He's fine. I'll pop up and check on him in the morning. I'll bring up some logs for his breakfast. And a basket to sleep in.'

'But you can't just leave me!' Ronald was horrified. 'I don't know what to *do*.'

'You don't have to do anything. He's asleep.'

'But what if he wakes up and tries flaming me again?'

'Do what I did. Threaten him with a slipper.'

'But I left my slippers down in the lab!'

'A rolled up newspaper, then. Just be firm. But I think he'll probably sleep through the night. I'm off. See you tomorrow.'

The second the door closed, Denzil came out of his sleepy trance. His head snapped round and he glowered at Ronald, who automatically ducked. He didn't flame, though. He bounded out of the toolbox, shot across the floor in a scrabble of talons and vanished under Ronald's bed. The last Ronald saw of him was the vanishing barbed tip of his tail.

'I say!' said Ronald, trying to be firm. 'Come out this minute!'

Silence. Ronald wondered whether to try using his Mystic Staff to poke him out.

Perhaps not.

He decided to sleep in the chair.

## Chapter Nine

# *Breakfast*

I t was the following morning and the echoes of the breakfast gong were still reverberating as Ronald dragged himself down the million stairs. He was aching in every limb. A chair is no place to sleep.

He had spent most of the night sitting bolt upright sniffing for smoke, eyes fixed worriedly on the darkness under the bed. He was cold too, when the fire in the hearth finally died. When he did drop off, he had terrible nightmares featuring flame, smoke and slow-motion running in chicken slippers.

He had finally woken in the grey light of dawn to the sight of Denzil glaring down balefully from the shelf, tail twitching. Some time in the small hours he must have emerged from under the bed, flown up and draped himself over

Ronald's piggy bank. It wasn't a great start to the day.

Ronald padded barefoot along the corridor leading to the Dining Hall. He had changed out of his ruined Robe of Mystery into his Other Robe, which he didn't much like. It was tight across the chest and covered with old stains. He'd had a go at brushing his singed Hat with his hairbrush, but it hadn't helped much. Up on the shelf, Denzil had watched his every move. He was glad to get out of the room.

Hattie was approaching from the other end of the corridor. She was carrying a basket in her arms. It was full of chopped firewood. A small pink blanket was neatly folded on top. They met just outside the Dining Hall door.

'How's it going?' she whispered. 'Did he stay in the toolbox?'

'No,' muttered Ronald. 'The second you left he shot under the bed. I had to sleep in the chair. I'm not going to get in a bed with a Dragon under it, am I? It's a fire hazard.'

'Is he still there?'

'No. I wish he was.'

'Where is he, then?'

'Up on the shelf,' said Ronald grimly.

'What – he flew? You saw him do it?'

'No, but he's up there. Sprawled all over my piggy bank. Glaring down at me with his tail twitching.'

'Guarding your treasure,' said Hattie. 'That makes sense.'

'But he's not supposed to guard it from *me!* I need the tenner, I want to send off for new slippers.'

'I'll get it for you. Stop fussing.'

'And he won't let me go near the sink.'

'Probably nervous of water. No more flaming, I hope?'

'Not yet.'

'You see? He's learning. I'll take him up his new basket, he'll like that. And some logs. He's probably ready for breakfast.'

'Me too,' said Ronald. He hadn't eaten a morsel the previous day, and he was ravenous.

'Go and eat, then. Don't be long, though. I've got work to do.'

'Right.' Ronald opened the door, glad to be relieved of the responsibility.

The Dining Hall had a long, white-clothed table running the length of one wall. On top was a line of silver dome-covered platters containing sausages, bacon, eggs, black pudding and all the other makings for a full cooked breakfast. There were plates of muffins, scones and pastries. There was toast.

There was marmalade. There was everything. Butler the butler stood to attention by the vast feast, armed with a coffee pot, ready to attend to the Wizards' every need. A couple of kitchen maids were standing by with jugs of juice.

And the Wizards? Well, they were eating.

They sat on either side of a central table. On one side sat Frank the Foreteller, Dave the Druid and Harold the Hoodwinker. On the other sat Fred the Flameraiser, Gerald the Just and Alf the Invisible, who was represented by a piled plate and cutlery that spookily moved by itself. Bits of sausage kept rising in the air and vanishing from the end of the fork.

Nobody was talking. For Wizards, eating is a competitive business. The only sounds were the clinking of cutlery, the disgusting noise of mass chewing and the occasional demand for salt, pepper, mustard and chilli sauce. The salt shaker, pepper grinder, mustard pot and sauce bottle moved of their own accord, whizzing up and down the table and dispensing their contents on to plates.

Ronald walked in. There was no chair for him at the table, of course. As usual, he would have to eat standing up. There was another golden statue of Mervyn the Mighty just inside the door. It had a usefully crooked elbow. He usually balanced his plate on that.

Frank was on his third helping of fry-up. Dave was keeping pace, mouthful by mouthful. Harold was vigorously mashing up beans with a fork. He couldn't eat chewy things on account of having no teeth. Opposite, Fred, Gerald and Alf were showing no signs of flagging.

Ronald walked to the side table, helped himself to a plate and began peering under the silver domes. Butler watched, and so did the kitchen maids. None of them offered to serve him. The Wizards ignored him. Ronald-baiting came later, in the Lounge, after toast and marmalade and the fourteenth cup of coffee.

He piled his plate high with sausages, bacon, eggs, chips, beans, fried bread and mushrooms, adding a cherry tomato as a token gesture toward his five a day. He helped himself to cutlery, walked over to Mervyn's statue, placed his plate on the useful elbow and began to eat.

From behind came the scraping of a chair. Dave the Druid stood up.

'Right, bit of a break before the next course. I'll just pop along and collect the newspaper.'

Dave always got the paper. By rights it was Brenda's

job, but Dave considered that bending down to pick it up from the mat was a nice bit of morning exercise.

*The Daily Miracle* had recently been taken over by a brand new paper, called *Witchway World*. It contained a great many flattering articles about Wizards. Dave's brother-in-law was the editor. He tended to be biased.

Butler hastened to remove Dave's plate. This was Ronald's chance. He snatched up his own plate and made for Dave's empty chair.

'Morning, young Ronald,' said Gerald, through a mouthful of sausage. 'You're quite a stranger. We missed you at all the meals yesterday.'

'I was in the Library,' said Ronald.

'The Library?' cut in Fred. 'What – *reading*?'

The Wizards all paused in their eating and stared at Ronald. He wasn't known as a reader.

'I see you're wearing your Other Robe of Mystery this morning,' observed Frank. 'A few nasty stains here and there. Seen a few breakfasts, that. Could tell some tales, that Robe.'

'More like a Robe of *History*,' said Alf wittily. Everyone chuckled except Ronald.

'Still no shoes, I notice,' said Fred. 'And what's with the charred Hat? Did you get that *reading*? Did your head catch fire, with all that knowledge streaming in?'

'What were you reading *about*?' asked Alf.

'Nothing special,' mumbled Ronald, shovelling in bacon.

'Would you like some chilli sauce with that?' enquired Frank.

'No, thank you. I'm not fond of chilli.'

'Nonsense. A good fry-up always needs chilli sauce.' Frank snapped his fingers at the sauce bottle, which was at the far end of the table. '*Sauce for young Ronald!*'

The bottle gave a little start, zoomed down the table, banged into Ronald's plate and upended itself. A river of red hot sauce poured all over his eggs and formed into a lake at the bottom of his plate.

Just at that moment, Dave returned with the newspaper tucked beneath his arm.

'Right, young Ronald. I'll have my chair back now.'

With a sigh, Ronald stood up. Butler snatched away his swimming plate and set down a nice, new, clean one for Dave.

'Can I get you something, sir?' he enquired.

'Just a couple of muffins,' said Dave, sitting down and opening the paper to the first page. 'And a Danish pastry. And three crumpets. No jam. Need to watch the waistline.'

Ronald wandered over to the side table and helped himself to a slice of toast. He was thinking about

Denzil. How was Hattie getting on? He hoped she'd managed to recover the tenner.

'Good heavens!' At the table, Dave was staring open-mouthed at the front page of the paper. 'See the headline? I don't *believe* it!'

'What?' came the interested chorus.

'The Gold Crested Wallaroon's back! Spotted yesterday, flying in from the South! Making for its usual nesting site on the cliffs over Sludgehaven!'

Great excitement greeted this announcement. Knives and forks clattered on to plates as the Wizards sat back in their chairs, breakfast forgotten.

'Shurely not!' That was Harold the Hoodwinker. 'The Gold Creshted Wallaroon? Amazhing!'

'*There's* a golden opportunity for some ambitious young Wizard to seize his chance!' cried Frank. 'Not me, of course. No more quests for me. My heroic days are over.'

'What does it say, Dave?' asked Gerald. 'Any more information?'

'Not much. More news to follow in tomorrow's edition.'

'Hear that, young Ronald?' shouted Fred. 'The Gold Crested Wallaroon's returned!'

'So?' said Ronald. He had never even heard of the Gold Crested Wallaroon.

'So it's incredible news! The first sighting for a hundred years! Bird watchers from far and wide are descending in their hordes!'

'Oh, right,' said Ronald uninterestedly. He couldn't care less about some boring old bird. He was much more concerned about the Dragon upstairs.

The Wizards began chatting excitedly, begging Dave to pass the paper so that they could have a look for themselves.

Ronald swallowed the last of his toast and hurried out.

Up in his room, he was greeted by a scene of cosy domesticity. The fire blazed in the hearth. Hattie was sitting cross-legged on the floor next to the basket. Denzil was sitting on the pink blanket, taking small, polite bites out of the log that she held out for him. His jaws chewed methodically, making a noise like a small rock crusher.

'Had your breakfast?' asked Hattie as Ronald entered, puffing as usual on account of the stairs.

'Kind of. How's he doing?'

'Wonderfully,' said Hattie. 'He loves his basket. And see how nicely he's eating. I got him to light your fire, see? He came down off the shelf without a murmur, didn't you, Denzil? Here's your aunty's tenner, by the way.'

She waved a crumpled ten pound note at Ronald, who took it.

'Thanks.'

'Have you written to thank her?'

'No. Not yet.'

'Well, you should.'

'I will. I *will*.'

'It's just that another card's arrived.' Hattie pointed to the desk, where a second card was propped in front of the first one. You could tell that the message was frosty, because the card was rimmed with tiny icicles.

'Oh,' said Ronald. 'When did that get here?'

'Two minutes ago. There was a zipping noise, and there it was on the desk.'

'Yes, well, Magic's quicker than the post.' Reluctantly, Ronald picked up the chilly card.

It said:

*Still no news regarding the ten pound note I sent for your birthday. In my day, people always wrote quaint things we called 'thank you letters' upon receiving a gift.*

*Your aunt.*

Ronald gave a sigh and dropped it before his fingers got frostbite.

'I'd better go.' Hattie rose to her feet. 'I'll take the toolbox, he doesn't need it now.'

'You can stay a bit longer, can't you?' asked Ronald, alarmed. 'What's the rush?'

'I've got things to do.'

'But he'll be back up on my piggy bank the moment you leave.'

'No he won't. It's empty. No treasure to guard.'

'But what if he wants to – to – you know?'

'I thought you'd read about Dragons,' said Hattie. 'I thought you were an expert. I thought you'd read an entire encyclopedia.'

'It didn't say anything about that, though.'

'Well,' said Hattie, 'I shouldn't worry. I tried giving him water in your tooth mug, but he turned his nose up. If he doesn't drink, he won't need to piddle, will he? And I reckon he'll just digest the log in his tummy. All that'll come out is gas.'

They both stared down at Denzil. His stomach was indeed making explosive sounds. He looked up at Hattie and wagged his tail.

'Lovely,' said Ronald. 'Something else to look forward to.'

'Well, I'm off down to the lab.' Hattie picked up her toolbox. 'I need to collect my tools and release the rabbits. If I've got time, I'll tackle the floor. Shall I remember you to the Demon?'

'No.'

'Do you want your slippers back? If there's anything left of them?'

'No, thank you. I'm ordering new ones from the Catalogue.'

'I'll pop up later to see how you're getting on. Be firm, mind.'

The door closed, and Ronald and Denzil were alone together. There was quite a longish pause.

'You can come out now,' said Ronald. 'I suppose.'

Denzil rose, stretched out his bat wings, and stepped out of the basket, yellow eyes fixed on Ronald. He crept forward a couple of steps, then stopped. He sank to the floor, going all long and low.

'There's a good boy,' said Ronald. He stretched out an encouraging hand. 'Come to be friends, have you? Shake a claw?'

Denzil avoided the encouraging hand. Instead, he went for the other one. The one that was holding the ten pound note! His jaws opened, snapped shut and once again Ronald found himself short of a tenner. The note in his mouth, Denzil flapped up on to Ronald's nice clean bed, dropped it and sat on it.

'Bad boy!' scolded Ronald. '*Not* on the bed! Get off!'

Denzil remained defiantly right where he was.

'Off!' ordered Ronald. 'Give me my money!'

Denzil growled. There were gurgling sounds coming from his belly.

'All right!' snapped Ronald. 'All right, have it your own way. I'm telling Hattie, though.'

Angrily, he crossed to his desk, pulled out the chair and sat down with his back turned. He opened the drawer and took out a pen and paper. It was time to write to Aunt Sharkadder.

*dere arnty*, wrote Ronald. Spelling wasn't his strong point. *thak you for the munny*.

And there he was stuck. He ought to write something else, but what? Should he mention the umbrella? Perhaps not, she might buy him another one. The missing Certificate? No, definitely not that. He had to think.

It didn't help that he was horribly aware of two orbs of yellow hatred boring holes in his back. It made it difficult to concentrate.

*i hop you are well*, wrote Ronald, then crossed it out. Of course she was well. She was a Witch. On the rare occasions that Witches get sick, they treat themselves with their own remedies. He didn't want to imply that hers might not work.

He screwed up the letter and began again.

*dere arnty thak you . . .*

From behind came a terrible noise. It was an

explosive, gassy hiss and it was accompanied by the most appalling odour that had ever met his nostrils, including all the smells down in the Laboratory.

Ronald whirled around, choking. Denzil sat quietly on his bed. He was staring at Ronald in something like proud triumph, mixed with relief.

It was the beginning of a trying time.

## Chapter Ten

# A Trying Time

Ronald tried. Oh yes, he tried. He tried shouting and he tried wheedling. He tried a rolled up newspaper, but Denzil snatched it away and ate it. He tried feeding Denzil with logs like Hattie did, but he turned his nose up. He preferred eating coal from the fireplace, which he dragged all over the floor. When Ronald's back was turned, he flew up on the desk, swallowed the unfinished thank you letter, crunched up the pen, then went back on the bed and refused to get off. He only went in his basket when Hattie was in the room. He didn't pass gas in front of her either. He saved that for Ronald.

The second night, Ronald couldn't face the chair and decided to risk sleeping in his bed. Denzil waited until he had settled, then flapped up and strolled all over the bedspread, leaving sooty footmarks. He waddled to the bottom and scrabbled around in circles, making himself a kind of nest, then slumped heavily right on top of Ronald's feet. He wasn't a quiet sleeper either. He wriggled and sighed and snored. Little explosions came from his stomach. Every time Ronald turned over, he hissed. Several times during the night, he got up to lick soot out of the chimney. Ronald could hear him slobbering and slurping. It was horrible.

Ronald complained about this to Hattie.

'Look at it,' he said. 'Look at the *mess*! Soot and talon holes and those awful green scales. I think he's moulting. And he's so restless at night.'

'You shouldn't allow him on the bed,' said Hattie. Denzil was rubbing lovingly around her ankles, purring.

'I don't *allow* him,' said Ronald irritably. 'He just does it.'

'That's because you're not firm. In your basket, Denzil! Lie down!' Obediently, Denzil trotted back to his basket, climbed in and lay down. 'Good boy. You love your basket, don't you?'

'No he doesn't,' snapped Ronald. 'He only goes in it when you're around. The rest of the time he's everywhere he shouldn't be, driving me insane.

Gnawing at my bed legs. Helping himself to coal. Hissing whenever I trip over him. Eating my private correspondence. I daren't leave the room. I'm scared of the damage he'll do.'

'He needs exercise,' said Hattie. 'He's bored. We should open the window and let him have a proper fly.'

'Good idea!' said Ronald. Well, it was. Maybe Denzil would fly away and never come back.

'Not right now, though,' said Hattie, reading his mind. 'I've got a boiler to lag. I want to be here when you do it. He'll come back to me. We'll try it when he's more settled. Cheer up. Isn't it lunchtime?'

It was. But Ronald had no appetite for lunch. Or for tea, or supper, or any meals really. The Wizards were still going on and on about the Gold Crested Wallaroon, who apparently was building a nest at the top of some tree somewhere. Ronald didn't know what all the fuss was about. He had other things on his mind. At mealtimes, he skulked around until the Wizards left the Dining Hall then raced in and grabbed himself a selection of individual jams and a handful of sugar lumps before the servants could clear them away.

He was petrified of leaving Denzil alone in case fire broke out. In all fairness, Denzil didn't flame unless Hattie gave him permission. He lit the fire on

her command and made a nice, neat job of lighting the candle. But he sprayed sparks whenever he sneezed. The new rug was already pitted with little black holes.

The second time that Hattie recovered his tenner, Ronald didn't take any chances. He put it straight into his pocket. Denzil gave it up without a single protest. Hattie rewarded him with Ronald's sugar lumps, leaving Ronald with nothing to sustain him apart from the little individual pots of jam. It was quite sickening. As was the jam.

Later that day, a third postcard arrived from Sharkadder. This one arrived with an angry *whoosh*. Poisonous-looking acid green flames were playing around the edge. Ronald didn't dare pick it up. He read it standing well back, which was easy because it was written in large black capitals.

It said:

### *I AM STILL WAITING.*

When evening was drawing in, Ronald humbly presented himself to Mrs Swipe and asked if his Cloak of Darkness and shoes were ready. They were. He thanked her profusely. She sniffed and banged the door in his face.

He put his shoes back on in the corridor. They felt a bit stiff, but he wasn't sorry to say goodbye to his feet.

He hurried back up to his room, opening the door with caution. Denzil's latest habit was lying in wait and launching himself at Ronald's back the second he entered the room. There he would cling, talons digging in, breathing hot, volcanic breath down Ronald's neck while Ronald danced around trying in vain to dislodge him. He had to be literally *scraped* off, using a corner of the wardrobe.

Denzil wasn't in attack mode this time. He was back on Ronald's bed, snoozing.

Carefully, Ronald hung the Cloak on a hanger in the wardrobe. The Laundry had done a surprisingly good job. In fact, it looked as good as new. He wouldn't feel so bad about using some of his birthday money to pay off the final instalment now. Hopefully, there would be enough left over to order some new socks and a decent pair of slippers.

Leaving Denzil still sleeping, he went back down to see if Hattie was around. He was rather hoping she would come up so that he could casually slip on the Cloak. She had never actually seen him looking his best. There was no sign of her. He walked along to Old Crabbit's room to enquire, but Old Crabbit was pretending to be asleep, despite his vigorous knocking.

When Ronald returned, he found to his horror that Denzil had discovered a new amusement. The wardrobe door was swinging open and the Cloak was lying on the floor in a crumpled heap. Denzil sat on top, kneading and drooling, talons making hundreds of little holes in the velvet.

Ronald snatched it away, hung it up and slammed the wardrobe door. Denzil hissed at him and flew back up to the shelf, landing with a thump. The shelf sagged. He was getting heavy.

Ronald went back down and once again walked along to Old Crabbit's room. He hammered on the door.

'Who is it?' came the feeble response. 'I'm in bed.'

'Me. Ronald the Magnificent.'

'Oh.' The voice didn't sound so feeble this time. 'What do *you* want?'

'Is Hattie there? I'd like a word.'

'No.'

'Well, do you know where she is?'

'No. Go away, I'm a sick man.'

'What's up?' asked Hattie's voice, from behind him. 'Problems?'

'He's only ruined my Cloak,' snapped Ronald.

'He got it out of the wardrobe and sat on it with his wretched talons going in and out.'

'Kneading,' said Hattie wisely. 'Cats do that. It's a comfort thing.'

'But I still haven't *paid* for it! I'd like you to come up and tell him off. He takes no notice of me. He's nearly gnawed through one of the bed legs and I think he might have eaten my hairbrush. I can't find it, anyway.'

'I can't come right now,' said Hattie. 'I promised to look at Brenda's spellophone. The dial's spun right off and she can't ring Pauline.'

'Well, thanks!' said Ronald. 'Thanks a *lot*. You're a great help, I must say.' And he stamped off back upstairs.

Denzil was still up on the shelf. When Ronald came in, his hackles rose, and he spat, long and hard.

'*Ptttthhhhhhtttt!*'

'That's quite enough from you!' snapped Ronald. He strode across the room, wrenched the curtain aside and flung the window wide open. Cool night air seeped in. High above, there sailed a full moon. 'Hey! Denzil! Fancy a fly?'

Denzil sat up and examined the open window. There was a gleam of interest in his yellow eyes.

'Come on, then,' urged Ronald, patting the window sill. 'It's all right, you're allowed. Hattie said.'

Denzil rose up on all four feet, unfolded his wings and flapped down on to the ledge. His long neck stretched out into the night air. His eyes were on the moon.

'Go on,' said Ronald. 'You know you want to.'

Denzil took a deep, deep breath. Then he extended his wings and leapt into the sky. Moonlight glinted on his green head – and he was gone!

'And don't come back!' yelled Ronald, banging the window shut.

Triumphantly, he pulled the curtain across. He'd done it! He'd got rid of Denzil! Hattie would be mad at him, but he'd say that he'd opened the window by mistake.

Humming to himself, he strolled to the sink and turned on the tap. For the first time in three days, he could actually clean his teeth. He made a big deal of it, with plenty of luxurious froth and a lot of thorough scrubbing. He washed his face. He squeezed a couple of spots in a leisurely way. Then he took off his Robe and pulled on his nightshirt. He heaped a few more coals on to the fire, blew out the candle, climbed into bed, snuggled down and instantly fell into a deep, blissful, Dragon free sleep.

In the middle of the night, he awoke screaming

to the sound of a window smashing, followed by a crushing weight descending on his chest.

Denzil had returned! It had clearly been raining, because he was soaking wet. He gave himself a hearty shake, splattering droplets all over Ronald. That was followed by a huge belch. He then waddled to the end of the bed, scattering glass shards, flopped down with a contented sigh and instantly began snoring. His stomach was churning loudly, obviously building up gas. Any minute now.

Ronald stuck his head under his pillow and tried not to breathe.

Something would have to be done.

Early next morning, Ronald was woken by a brisk knock on his door.

'Only me!' came Hattie's voice.

Denzil was up and off the bed in a shot. He squeezed into his basket, and sat really nicely. Quite the model little Dragon. Well, actually, not quite so little. Either the basket was shrinking, or he was growing. There was a certainly a lot less space.

'Suck up,' snarled Ronald. He swung his legs on to the floor and padded across to open the door, wishing that his nightshirt didn't have a kitten embroidered on the pocket (another present from Aunt Sharkadder). He hoped Hattie wouldn't notice.

'Cute kitten on your nightshirt,' said Hattie.

'Thank you,' said Ronald stiffly. 'It wasn't my choice.'

'I hear your window's smashed,' said Hattie. 'The courtyard's full of glass. Harold the Hoodwinker cut his foot.'

'Yes,' said Ronald. 'I opened it last night to get some air in.'

'I see,' said Hattie.

'Yes. I was a bit too firm closing it again.'

'I see.'

'Yes. I didn't want Denzil escaping.'

'I see.'

'Yes. That's how it got broken.'

'You're lying, aren't you?'

'Yes,' admitted Ronald. 'I am.' He gave a sigh. 'I let him out and hoped he'd never come back again. But he did. Straight through the window in the middle of the night. Gave me a terrible shock.'

'Hmm. Well, luckily I've got my toolbox.' Hattie's eyes went to Denzil, who was clawing his blanket, waiting eagerly for the word. 'Come on, then, big boy! Up you come!'

Joyfully, Denzil flew into her arms, licking her face with his long green tongue.

'Oh, for crying out loud,' muttered Ronald, disgusted.

'Whoah! Denzil!' laughed Hattie, staggering a bit. 'You're getting *heavy*. Down you go!' She set him on the floor, where he rolled over to have his tummy tickled.

They both looked down at him.

'You're right, you know,' said Ronald. 'He's growing. I'm not surprised, with all he's eating. He foraged for himself when he was out on his fly too. There were leaves stuck in his teeth.'

'He's just having a growth spurt,' said Hattie.

'You can say that again. Look at him. He's almost doubled in size in a couple of days. Come to think of it, there was something in the encyclopedia about Dragons growing quickly in the early stages.'

'No problem,' said Hattie, playfully rolling Denzil over with her foot. 'I'll get him a bigger basket.'

'What happens when he grows out of that?'

'Well, we don't know how big he'll end up. Let's worry about it when it happens.'

'This is a small room,' said Ronald. 'I need to worry about it now.'

'Well, go and do it somewhere else. I've got to fix your window. Then I'll play with him with string for ten minutes. Hopefully that'll tire him out. Off you go. And take that dirty old Robe with you and put it in the laundry basket.'

'All right, if you don't want my company,' said Ronald, rather sulkily. 'If you'd sooner *play* with some stupid *Dragon*.'

'Sssh! He understands everything you say, you know.'

Ronald snatched up his filthy Robe of Mystery from the corner where he'd thrown it and stormed out, banging the door behind him.

## Chapter Eleven

# Getting Rid of Denzil

Ronald stood in front of the Library door, examining the notice that was stuck on the front. It said:

**CLOSED UNTIL FURTHER NOTICE.**

His heart sank. His plan had been to consult the encyclopedia and see if there was anything about sending unwanted Dragons back where they came from. Basically, a sort of reverse Summoning. What would you call that? A Rejection? A Dismissal? Whatever it was called, Hattie wouldn't approve. But she didn't have to know.

'Well, if it isn't young Ronald,' said a voice. 'Here to do more *reading*, are we?'

Behind him was Dave the Druid with a copy of *Witchway World* beneath his arm.

'Yes, actually,' said Ronald.

'You missed breakfast this morning,' went on Dave. 'Hungry for knowledge, I expect?'

'Yes,' said Ronald. 'I am. But as you can see, the Library's closed.'

'Ah,' said Dave. 'Our delightful Miss Stickler. Run out of twigs, I imagine. She does from time to time. But if you're anxious for reading material, I just happen to have today's paper.'

'No, it's all right.'

'More news of the Wallaroon. Huge excitement in Sludgehaven. Massive tourist attraction. Here. Take it.'

'No, really.'

'Go on. It has a twelve-metre wingspan, you know. It can break a man's arm.'

'I thought that was swans.'

'Oh, the Wallaroon's much fiercer than a *swan*. No comparison. That's why nobody dares go near it, despite the obvious attraction of the egg.'

'What's attractive about its egg?'

'Well, it's solid gold, isn't it?'

'Is it?'

'Oh, yes. Worth a fortune. Go on, read all about it.' Dave thrust the paper at him. 'I insist.'

'All right. Thanks.' Ronald took the paper, shoved it under his arm and walked off.

'They say it's nesting!' shouted Dave. 'Laying the egg any day now! Solid gold!'

He was shouting at thin air.

Ronald descended the steps to the Laundry. The door was closed. Set outside was a big wicker basket, in which the Wizards were supposed to place their grubby washing. A stout-looking clip held the lid down. Wizardly garments have a habit of escaping when faced with the prospect of being washed by Mrs Swipe. Often at night, you would see an old shirt crawling up the stairs on its way back to its owner, or a furtive pair of grubby trousers lurking behind a statue, ready to make a run for it.

Ronald undid the clip and opened the lid. Wizards are not particularly clean in their habits, so it was currently empty. He was just about to throw in the Robe when a sudden, brilliant idea occurred to him.

So far, his efforts to get rid of Denzil hadn't worked. He wouldn't fly away. There was no way that he could be un-Summoned now the Library was closed. But what if . . . ?

'Yes,' muttered Ronald. 'Yes. It just might work.'

There was no one around. The Wizards would still be at breakfast in the Dining Hall. He threw in the Robe, slammed the lid shut, seized the basket by its handles – and ran! He charged back along the corridor, up the steps, along another corridor, up more stairs, and took the last flight of the million steps up to his room, three at a time.

He paused outside the door, gasping as always.

'Hattie?' he called. 'Are you in there?'

All was quiet. Basket in hand, he cautiously pushed open the door with his foot, prepared for the usual attack.

Denzil was asleep on the bed. He was really getting bigger. Definitely eating too much. Goodness knows what he had scoffed the night before. From the smell of the room, probably an entire wood, with a couple of small barns for pudding.

There was a new pane of glass in the window with a note propped against it. It said:

*All tired out with string. Should sleep for a bit now.*

Walking on tiptoe, Ronald sidled in. Carefully, trying not to rustle, he put the newspaper on his desk. Then he tiptoed across and placed the laundry basket next to the bed. Cautiously, he opened the lid, took out his Robe and threw it back in the corner. Holding his breath, he tiptoed to the wardrobe and opened the door.

There wasn't much in there, apart from his Other Robe, his Cloak of Darkness and the suit he had worn for the interview. The tie – a blue, spotty one – was draped around the shoulders. Ronald pulled it off, trying not to rattle the hanger.

Tie in hand, he tiptoed across to Denzil's basket and picked up the pink blanket, which was covered with small green scales. He gave it a disgusted little shake. On the bed, Denzil stopped snoring. Ronald froze. But all was well. He started again.

Holding both tie and blanket, Ronald tiptoed to the bed. This was the moment. Timing was all.

He leapt!

Denzil's head jerked up – but too late! In seconds, the tie was wound tightly around his jaws and secured with a knot. The blanket came down over him, hands gripped his sides, and he suddenly found himself being borne through the air and plonked in some sort of container. Automatically he tried flaming, but his jaws were muzzled, so he couldn't. Smoke came out of his ears and gas came out of – well, you don't want to know. Furiously, he struggled out of the blanket and stared up into Ronald's triumphant face.

It was the last thing he saw before the lid went down.


The lobby was deserted. Brenda was off somewhere having one of her many coffee breaks.

Holding the bucking, heaving basket in his hands, Ronald hurried to the main door. He had changed out of the nightshirt and was wearing his Other Robe, his Cloak of Darkness (complete with holes and dribble stains) and his charred Hat of Knowledge.

He set down the heavy basket. Little tendrils of smoke were trickling through the wicker. The lid kept jerking up and down as Denzil thrashed around inside, but the stout clip was holding. Ronald reached to open the door.

A stern voice rapped, 'Just *where* do you think you're going?'

It was Hattie. She had a habit of coming up behind when he was least expecting it. What a disaster! Caught red-handed.

Inside the basket, Denzil stopped thrashing, settled down and waited for rescue like a good boy.

'Nowhere,' said Ronald. 'Walking.'

'With the laundry basket?'

'I'm taking a picnic.'

'Oh, you are, are you? What sort of food?'

'Jam.' Ronald cast his eyes down to the little trickles of smoke coming from the basket. 'Smoked jam. Like smoked ham, only – um – jammier.'

'Rubbish. You've got Denzil in there, haven't you?'

'No. Well, all right, yes. I thought he'd like some fresh air.'

'Liar. You're going to dump him, aren't you? I always know when you're fibbing.'

Ronald gave in. 'OK,' he said. 'You're right. I am.'

'Where?'

'Nowhere special.'

In fact, the plan had been to dump Denzil in Goblin Territory – a bleak, windswept place whence few returned. He would leave the basket under a tree with a note saying *Free Dragon*. What the Goblins would do with a Dragon he had no idea. Poke it with a stick? Take turns riding on it? Put it in a football team? Who cared, as long as it never came back.

'Well, I'm surprised at you,' said Hattie. 'Surprised and disappointed.'

'Look,' said Ronald. 'I can't keep him in my room

any more. Look at him, he's getting huge. And more horrible by the second.'

'Ssshh. He can understand everything you say, you know.'

'No, he can't. Even if he can, I don't care. He's dreadful. I just don't want him.'

'Then it's your responsibility to find him a loving home.'

'*You* take him home and love him, then.'

'I'm not *at* home, am I? I'm here. But I clearly can't trust you with him.' Hattie picked up the laundry basket. 'I'm putting him in the woodshed for now. You need time out from each other. You can both think about your behaviour.'

'Good!' snarled Ronald. 'Glad to see the back of him!'

And he stomped back up to his room.

## Chapter Twelve

# A Journey with Fish

There was another postcard waiting on the desk. This one was seriously on fire. It burned furiously, little red flames licking around the edge and singeing the desk beneath.

Ronald hastened to the sink and threw a glass of water over it. It was horribly charred, but he could just about make out the last line.

It said:

### *AND MAY YOU NEVER DARKEN MY DOOR AGAIN!!!!*

He would really have to reply this time. If he wasn't careful, she would show up in person and demand the tenner back. But not now. First, he wanted to relax a bit. Put his feet up. Enjoy having his room to himself again, without a Dragon in it. Have a look at the newspaper.

He dropped the soggy postcard into the wastebasket, picked up the paper, threw himself on the bed and examined the screaming headline.

## BIRD ABOUT TO LAY EGG!

*Crowds have gathered at the site of the tallest tree on the cliffs at Sludgehaven, where the legendary Gold Crested Wallaroon is nesting. The Mayor of Sludgehaven said, 'For reasons of health and safety, the public is warned not to approach it. We would all like a solid gold egg, who wouldn't, but the risks are too great. The Wallaroon is a bird which can only be restrained by Magic. Maybe a bold, agile, heroic young Wizard might succeed in frightening it off with Finger Sparkles, but otherwise . . .*

Ronald read on.

The woodshed was situated at the back of the Clubhouse, tucked into a corner of the Wizards' overgrown allotment. Gardening is not high on a Wizard's list of priorities.

'Here we are, Denzil,' said Hattie, pulling open the

door. 'Your new home. You'll like it, it's bigger than Ron's room.'

Denzil stared into the shed, eyes gleaming and tail wagging to and fro. He was gazing at the logs. Massive, heaped mountains of logs, stretching from floor to ceiling.

'In you go,' said Hattie. 'I'll be back later. I suggest you have a quiet think about things. You're not making life easier for yourself, you know.'

Denzil waddled in willingly. He was clearly happy to bunk down anywhere but with Ronald.

The door closed. The lock clicked, and he was alone in the dark. He waited until Hattie's footsteps died away.

He began on the first log.

Ronald lay on the bed, thinking. Thinking about a golden egg.

It would solve all his money problems. He could sell it on Magimart, the Wizardly equivalent of eBay. Start a bidding war. There must be thousands of Wizards out there who would pay a fortune for such a rare thing.

He would be able to pay off the Cloak and order loads more stuff from the Catalogue. Socks. A manly umbrella. A decent pair of slippers. In fact, a whole new wardrobe. Thanks to Denzil, everything he possessed was burnt, full of holes or dribbled on. He could get a new Hat! New shoes! New everything!

There was another reason why he could do with the egg. This was the whole Fame thing. Fame, stardom, pictures in the paper. He would be a real celebrity! The Wizards would respect him for once. He would bring glory to the Clubhouse. They might buy him a chair. Although, of course, he'd be rich enough to buy his own chair, wouldn't he? A golden one, with a tasselled cushion.

Best of all, he would be able to pay someone to take on Denzil. Someone somewhere must run a shelter for homeless Dragons. With money in his pocket, new clothes and Denzil gone, his worries would be over.

He checked the article again.

*Maybe a bold, agile, heroic young Wizard might succeed in frightening it off with Finger Sparkles.*

Well. He could do those, couldn't he? After all, he had managed to Summon a Dragon. Finger Sparkles were small fry compared to that. He was definitely improving. He had demonstrated that he could be bold. He was reasonably agile. And heroic? Well – why not? Heroes didn't necessarily need muscles. Sometimes, quite small people stood up to huge giants and defeated them armed only with cunning, determination and, of course, confidence.

He could do it, couldn't he? Yes. He could. He could and he would.

He debated whether to discuss the new plan with Hattie. Perhaps not. He wasn't in her good books right now. She might try to put him off. No, he would keep it a secret. It would be so much more impressive if he arrived back home to a triumphant hero's welcome, brandishing a golden egg. He might even buy her a bunch of flowers or something, to say thank you for helping out with Denzil.

Or maybe he wouldn't. He was still smarting a bit from the last telling off.

He would think about that later. But right now, there was no time to be lost.

Craig the fish man was sitting in the driver's seat of his little white van, about to start the engine. He had just completed his last delivery of the day, which was to the Wizards' Clubhouse. Craig came every week, on a Friday. The Wizards bought in bulk, so there wasn't much left in the back of his van. Just a large, annoyed crab that was too tough to cook and a pile of particularly ugly, bony fish with teeth and weird feelers that nobody liked the look of. Despite being on ice, they smelled to high heaven.

Craig set his woolly hat straight, turned the key, put his foot down and was just about to pull away when there came the sound of running footsteps. A head topped with a pointy Hat loomed at the window.

Craig wound it down and said, 'Yes, mate?'

'Could I possibly beg a lift?' panted Ronald. 'I need to get to Sludgehaven in a hurry.'

'No problem, mate,' said Craig easily. 'You'll have to ride in the back, though. Boss don't like me taking passengers.'

'Right,' said Ronald. He hurried around to the back of the van and threw open the doors. 'Oh.'

'Sorry about the fish,' called Craig. 'Cheap job lot.'

'And – er – the crab?'

'Just keep yer toes away. It'll be a bit nippy in there, in more ways than one. I hope you're dressed up warm.'

'Ron?' called Hattie. 'Are you in there?' She knocked on the door.

Silence.

'Ron? Stop sulking and open up!'

More silence.

She opened the door. The room was empty.

Ronald's shape was outlined on the bedspread. On the pillow lay a crumpled newspaper.

Hattie gave a sigh. He was probably in the Library, looking up anti-summoning spells. She had a feeling that getting him and Denzil to bond was a lost cause.

Oh, well.

She picked up the paper, folded it and stuffed it in the pocket of her overalls. Maybe she'd get a minute to glance at the headlines later.

In the meantime, there was work to be done.

'Where d'you want dropping off, mate?' came Craig's voice from the front of the van.

'W-where are we?' shouted Ronald, though chattering teeth.

'Up on the cliffs. Just about to go down to Sludgehaven.'

'This'll d-d-do. Just let me out quickly, w-will you?'

It had been an excruciatingly bumpy drive over the mountains. And cold? Cold wasn't the word. For two whole hours Ronald had crouched shivering in a corner, surrounded by melting ice and stinking, slithery fish while his breath froze in the air. The tough old crab had kept eyeing his feet and clashing its horrible claws. He was desperate to get out.

The back doors opened and he leapt into the light

with a glad cry, scattering fish. His frozen ankles gave way and he landed heavily with a crunch, like a falling stalactite.

'Bit chilly in there, was it?' said Craig. 'I did warn you.'

'Y-yes,' said Ronald. 'F-f-freezing.'

'Well, I'd best be getting off.'

'Y-y-yes. Th-th-thanks for the l-l-lift.'

'No problem, mate.' Craig gave a cheery thumbs up, climbed back in the van and drove away.

Ronald picked himself up and tried to rub some life back into his arctic limbs. Then he stared around.

He was indeed on the clifftop. Up above, seagulls wheeled in the reddening sky. Far below could be seen the roofs of Sludgehaven. Its famous pier stretched out into the sea, where a few minuscule fishing boats bobbed. On the horizon, the sun was going down.

On the cliff itself, there was little to be seen apart from a clump of windblown trees growing right by the edge. One of them was much taller than the others. There was something at the top. It looked like – yes! A large, untidy nest.

So. This, clearly, was the nest of the Wallaroon. But where were the crowds? The huge, excited crowds, armed with cameras and binoculars? The paper had said that the nest was a massive tourist attraction, but not a soul was to be seen. Weird. Come to think of it, where was the Wallaroon? It was supposed to be a big bird, but as far as he could see, the distant nest looked deserted. Perhaps it had gone for a bite to eat. Of course. That was it. It had flown off, taking the excited crowds with it. Leaving the solid gold egg alone and unprotected!

Perfect timing. At last, luck was on his side. He wouldn't even have to use his Finger Sparkles.

Ronald brushed the last of the icicles off his Hat, shook a fish from his sleeve and set out for the trees.

The tallest tree was, as might be expected, the one nearest the edge. It rose up, up, up. The lower branches shielded the nest from sight. But it was up there. Now all he had to do was climb.

Ronald wasn't bad at shinning up trees. When he was younger, he was regularly chased up them by bigger boys. The experience would come in handy.

He removed his Cloak of Darkness, folded it and set it on the ground. It reeked of fish. He took off his battered Hat and placed it on top. Then he took a deep breath, spat on his hands, reached for the lowest branch – and began climbing.

Back at the Clubhouse, Hattie had finished her last job of the afternoon, which was gluing back Mervyn's nose, which had snapped off the statue on the landing. She was looking forward to putting her feet up with a mug of tea and a sandwich. First, though, she had to check on Denzil.

She packed away her tools, slipped out the back door and made her way down to the bottom of the allotment.

All was quiet in the woodshed.

She opened the door. A terrible, *terrible* smell wafted out.

'Oh no!' said Hattie. 'Oh, Denzil! You bad, *bad* boy!'

## Chapter Thirteen

# Up a Tree

Climbing was harder than Ronald remembered. The tree trunk was straight and smooth, with no useful forks where he could rest. The side branches were thin and bendy, with long gaps between them. He didn't so much shin as stretch, haul, cling on trembling, then stretch, haul, cling and tremble again.

He didn't dare look down. He didn't look up, either. He was afraid of seeing how much further he had to go. Out at sea, the sun dipped below the horizon.

Sweat dripped off the end of his nose. Moss and little bits of tree bark rained on his shoulders and got into his eyes. His hands were full of splinters and all the strength was leaving his arms. The wind was getting stronger the higher he climbed. It felt like the swaying tree was about to keel over and plunge down the cliff on to black, jagged rocks at any minute.

He climbed on. Stretch, haul, cling, tremble. Stretch, haul, cling, tremble. Would it never end?

Well, yes. Most things do.

He was nearly at the top now, where the trunk was really thin. Just above him, the tree forked – and in the fork, he could see the underside of the nest. With a dry mouth, he gripped the last bit of trunk, wrapped his knees around and pulled himself up. Stretch, heave – and he was there!

Eagerly, he raised his chin over the edge of the nest and stared down.

There was no golden egg. Instead, there was a sealed envelope. What was this?

Carefully, Ronald reached over and picked it up. He hooked an arm around the trunk and opened it with shaking fingers. Inside was a single sheet of paper, with the Clubhouse masthead at the top. Right in the middle, in block capitals, were three words.

### HAPPY MERVYN DAY!

He'd been tricked.

Ronald let the sheet of paper go. It fluttered away on the wind.

He couldn't believe it. The whole thing was a set-up. There was no Gold Crested Wallaroon. There was no golden egg. The Wizards must have bribed the editor of *Witchway World* who, come to think of it, was Dave the Druid's brother-in-law. It was all an elaborate prank – and he had fallen for it.

Up close, the nest didn't even look like a real bird's nest. It was woven from plastic straws, which the Wizards had obviously filched from the kitchen. That meant that Butler and the kitchen staff were in on the joke.

Ronald clung there, swaying. Now what? It was true that as a kid, he had been good at climbing up trees. But there was one thing he'd forgotten.

He was rubbish at getting back down.

It was morning in the Clubhouse. Hattie was doing her first job of the day, which was walking around with a sack, emptying the bins. She hadn't slept well the night before.

The problem, as usual, was Denzil. He had consumed an entire shed full of logs. Every last one. The result was catastrophic.

The eating orgy had brought on another major growth spurt. He was no longer the size of a coffee table. He was more like a small pony. So large, he'd have trouble squeezing out of the door. Stretched out, the tips of his wings now touched the walls on both sides. And then, of course, there was the digestive process. All that churning and gassy stomach explosions. Right now he was slumped in the empty shed, looking sad because he'd been told off and had a tummyache. Well, it served him right.

Hattie paused at the statue of Mervyn by the front door. His lightning bolt was glued back on. The lobby was deserted. No sign of Brenda. Hattie glanced around, fished the paper from her pocket and straightened it out. She'd been working really hard over the last few days. No one would begrudge her two minutes, surely? She leaned against Mervyn and began to read.

### BIRD ABOUT TO LAY EGG!

*Crowds have gathered at the site of the tallest tree on the cliffs at Sludgehaven, where the legendary Gold Crested Wallaroon . . .*

She read to the end. Well, almost the end. She had to stop because the Wizards were coming downstairs in a noisy group, on their way to breakfast.

Hastily, Hattie folded the paper and slid behind Mervyn.

The Wizards seemed to be in a particularly jolly mood, laughing and chattering. She caught snatches of their conversation as they strolled by.

'Took long enough for him to take the bait, but he got there in the end . . .'

'Did you see him running for the fish van, though? Thought I'd die laughing . . .'

'Reckon he's up the tree yet?'

'Let's break out the crystal balls after breakfast. I'd love to see him right now . . .'

They passed on down the corridor, following the smell of frying fish. Well, it was Mervyn Day, when merry pranks were played, Mervyn's song was sung and fish and chips were eaten at every meal.

Hattie waited until they were gone, then stepped out from her hiding place.

'Oh, Ron,' she sighed. 'You *idiot*.'

Then she sprang into action.

In the woodshed, Denzil's ears pricked up at the sound of fast approaching footsteps. He knew he was in disgrace. He shouldn't have done what he did, but he hadn't been able to help himself. Locking a Dragon in a woodshed is like putting a vampire in charge of a blood bank.

The door opened and sunlight streamed in. It

was her! It was Hattie, come to forgive him! Denzil lumbered to his feet and put on his most piteous expression, hoping for a cuddle. What he got instead was a face full of Ronald's filthy old Robe of Mystery, which we last saw in the corner of his room.

'Smell, Denzil!' said Hattie urgently. 'It's Ronald!'

Denzil's nose wrinkled distastefully. He knew that. Dragons' noses are highly sensitive, although not many people know that.

'Out you come,' said Hattie. 'Hurry up!'

She grabbed him by the ears and tugged. Desperate to oblige, Denzil sucked in his tummy and pushed. Between them, they got him through the doorway – but only just. It was like trying to squeeze a sponge through a slotted spoon. One thing was certain. He wouldn't be going back in.

He wondered whether to roll over and paddle his feet or offer a claw. Rolling over was getting more difficult these days, so he went for the claw.

'Not now!' said Hattie. 'No time for games. Hold still, I'm getting on.'

To Denzil's surprise, she gripped his frill and hauled herself astride his back. She felt as light as a feather. He lowered the frill to make her more comfortable. This was new! What now?

'Right,' said Hattie into his ear. 'This is where you

earn your keep. Don't let me down.' She dangled Ronald's robe in front of his nose again. '*Up you go, Denzil! Find! Find Ronald!*'

Denzil crouched down – unfurled his wings – and sprang into the air!

At the top of the tree in Sludgehaven, Ronald perched rigidly in the fake straw nest. He had been there all night.

It had taken the last of his strength to clamber in. It was just big enough to take him, providing he kept his knees bent. He had sat down carefully – very, very carefully, making sure the balance was right – and there he had stayed, white-knuckled hands clutching the sides, trying not to wobble or think of what lay below.

He had seen the stars come out above. He had watched the distant pier lights wink out far, far below. He had felt the night breeze blowing in from the sea. He had heard the owls hooting. Bats came and went. A passing squirrel sat on his head and ate a nut, just for a laugh. At one point, a flock of migrating geese had paused overhead to examine him before flying on, honking with helpless mirth.

The long dark night crawled by and still he sat, face pale and head swimming, staring straight ahead into black space, ignoring the whirling stars, not daring to move a muscle. He couldn't even think. There was only one thought occupying his brain. It chased out all others.

*Must. Not. Move.*

It hadn't got any better when the stars finally went in and the sun rose. Now he could see again – and he didn't want to. He knew without looking that the climb down would be impossible. His limbs were too numb.

Imagine how he felt when he saw the tiny dot flying towards him! The dot that wasn't an owl, bat, goose or seagull. The dot that was, in fact, *a large green Dragon with a determined-looking girl on his back*!

Just when all seemed lost, the cavalry had arrived!

Ignoring his frozen limbs, Ronald sprang to his feet, waving wildly and shouting.

'Hattie! Denzil! Over here, boy!'

What happened next was a real shame. What happened was, he wobbled – lost his balance –

*And fell like a stone!*

## Chapter Fourteen

# *The Hero Returns*

**B**ack in the Clubhouse, the Wizards were in the Dining Hall, waiting for lunch. It was Mervyn Day, so that meant more fish and chips. There had been fish and chips for breakfast too. The Wizards hadn't even got up from the table. On Mervyn Day, meals flowed smoothly into each other, with the occasional break for Magical tricks, which were performed between courses.

'A toast to Mervyn, our glorious founder!' shouted Frank the Foreteller.

'To Mervyn!' roared the Wizards, clinking their mugs of tea.

'Shall we shing the shong now?' That was Harold the Hoodwinker, who mistakenly believed that he had a pleasant singing voice.

'Yes,' agreed Gerald the Just. 'This would seem to be a good time – *good grief* !' He jaw dropped open as he stared through the window. 'Are my eyes deceiving me? There appears to be a – *Dragon* coming in to land! And isn't that – yes, I do believe it is – it's got *young Ronald* on its back!'

Out in the courtyard, Denzil's talons skidded on the flagstones, raising sparks. Using his wings as brakes, he came to an emergency stop just before crashing into the ornamental fountain. He gave a snort, folded his wings and stood panting, tongue hanging out and steam rising from his heaving sides.

'Good boy,' said Hattie, giving him a pat. 'You did really well.' She slid off his back. 'Come on, Ron. Down you get.'

'Give me a minute,' said Ronald. 'Just a minute.'

He needed to sit for a moment. Try to collect his thoughts. Try to forget that heart-stopping moment when he fell out of the nest and focus instead on the bit when Denzil came swooping to the rescue, inserting himself between Ronald and the sharp rocks at the very last possible second! Oh, that agonising pain when he thumped on to the broad green back! He would have toppled off again if Hattie hadn't grabbed him. It would be a long time before he forgot about that.

Flying home had been no picnic either. Hattie was at the front and had Denzil's ears to cling on to. Ronald had nothing to hold but Hattie. He had wrapped his arms around her waist, shut his eyes and tried not to scream as the wind buffeted his cheeks and the countryside flashed by hundreds of metres below.

It had been cold too. He wasn't dressed for Dragon riding. His Cloak and Hat were long gone, abandoned at the foot of the tree. He had lost his shoes in the fall. His Other Robe, not that great at the best of times, was torn in a million places. Yes, the flight had been truly horrible.

But he was home. Home and in one piece. He wanted to savour the moment. Pick the flies out of his teeth. Get his nerves under control. Try to come up with an explanation about why he had arrived home on a Dragon. There would be questions asked about that. And there would be endless teasing, of course. The Wizards would never let him forget that he had been fool enough to fall for their latest, elaborate prank.

'Come on!' insisted Hattie. 'You can't stay there all day. Anyway, it looks like we've got company.'

The main door had opened. Wizards were hurrying

down the steps led by Frank the Foreteller. They were closely followed by Butler, the kitchen staff, Brenda, Mrs Swipe and the laundry girls, and even Old Crabbit. Miss Stickler was there too, hovering at the back. The entire Clubhouse had turned out to gawp at him.

Ronald slithered down from Denzil's back. This was it, then. Time to face the music.

'Flaming Fireballs!' puffed Frank, who was the first to arrive. His face was purple with the effort of running. 'What in the world is *that*, young Ronald?'

'My Dragon,' said Ronald. He was too tired to come up with any more lies.

'What a magnificent beast!' That was Alf the Invisible's voice, coming from Denzil's front end. Denzil stared at the air in puzzlement, then backed away, hissing.

'Sssh,' said Hattie, giving him a soothing pat. 'Calm down, there's a good boy.'

Obediently, Denzil stood still.

'By the powers, I do believe it's *trained*!' gasped Gerald.

'Did you shummon it *yourshelf*, boy?' enquired Harold. Everyone was clustering around Denzil, poking at his scales, lifting his ears and peering up his nose. To his credit, he was taking it quite well.

'Yes,' admitted Ronald. 'I did it in the lab a few days ago.'

'In the lab?' said Frank the Foreteller sharply. 'I hope you didn't disturb my experiment.'

'I might have, actually,' admitted Ronald. 'A complete accident, of course.'

'Give the lad some credit,' said Gerald. 'A Dragon Summoning. That's *serious* Magic. Most Dragons resent being summoned. Usually turn on you. Well, the one I got did. Couldn't do a thing with it, had to send it back.'

'Didn't know you had it in you, boy,' agreed Fred, knocking out his pipe on Denzil's side. Denzil extended his tongue, scooped up the burning ashes and stood munching them with pleasure.

'Where have you been keeping it?' Dave wanted to know.

'In my room. Until it got too big.'

'Why didn't you tell us?' asked Fred.

'Well – there's a No Pets rule, isn't there?' There fell an uncomfortable silence. Ronald stared at them. 'Well – *isn't* there?'

The Wizards shuffled their feet and avoided each other's eyes. None of them would admit it, but each had a secret pet that he kept in his room. Between them, they had a gold-plated rhino (Rex), a sequinned

aardvark (Archie), a flashing tiger (Timmy), a spark-
ling guinea pig (George), an invisible canary who
sang show tunes (Carol) and a duck called Dick who
quacked in Latin. All very interesting in their own way,
of course. But nothing like as impressive as a living,
breathing, almost full-scale, perfectly trained Dragon.

'Does it breathe fire?' enquired Alf, to change the
subject.

'Yes,' said Ronald. 'But I don't encourage it.'

'Well, young Ronald, you are to be congratulated,'
said Gerald. 'I rather think that we have underesti-
mated you. Gentlemen, we are in the presence of a
Dragon Master.'

Ronald found himself surrounded. Wizards were
slapping him on the back. Queuing up to shake his
hand. Telling him how clever he was. Butler was leading the kitchen staff in a round of polite applause.
Even Mrs Swipe was staring at him with something
like admiration. He felt a bit of a fraud. After all,
Hattie had done most of the work.

'Sorry about the prank, by the way,' said Frank.
'The business with the Wallaroon and the golden
egg and so on. Just our little joke for Mervyn Day.
Traditional to pick on the youngest. No hard feelings, eh? Go on, Gerald. Give it to him.'

'Here, lad,' said Gerald. 'Just a little something for

being a good sport.' He thrust a fat leather purse into Ronald's hand. 'We had a whip-round. Get yourself some new togs from that Catalogue you're so fond of. You're looking a bit threadbare these days.'

'Wow!' said Ronald. 'OK. Thanks.'

'Talking of Mervyn, ishn't it time we shang the shong?' said Harold.

'Indeed it is,' agreed Gerald. 'Stand to attention, everyone.'

And the Wizards removed their hats, placed one arm across their chests, and burst into song.

*'Mervyn! Mervyn!*
*No one more deservin',*
*Founder of the Club,*
*We sing to you today!*
*Great enchanter,*
*Beard as long as Santa,*
*Three cheers for Mervyn,*
*Hooray, hooray, hooray!'*

Everyone threw their hats in the air apart from Ronald, who didn't have one.

'Right, that's it,' said Dave. 'Back to lunch, everybody. Come on, young Ronald, fish and chips await! Butler, fetch the lad a chair! Least we can do, eh?'

Everyone surged towards the door, and in a very short space of time, the courtyard was almost empty. A Dragon was all very interesting, but lunch called.

Only Miss Stickler remained, standing on the top step.

'Well done, young man,' she called. 'Glad to see you learnt something. Don't forget to drop in the Certificate. I'm still waiting, you know.' And with that, she was gone.

Ronald was left alone. Now that he was no longer the centre of attention, Denzil had wandered off under the archway and was noisily tearing ivy off the wall, eyed nervously by the gargoyle overhead.

'Hattie?' called Ronald. He stared around. Where was she? He had forgotten all about her, what with all the fuss.

He suddenly spotted her coming around the side of the Clubhouse. She had changed out of her overalls and was wearing her brown cloak and carrying her basket. What was this?

'Where are you going?' asked Ronald, hurrying to meet her.

'Home,' said Hattie.

'What? Why?'

'Uncle Rube's up and about again. He's repainting the Mervyns. My work is done.'

'But you can't – I mean, what about – you can't leave me with Denzil! He hates me!'

'Oh, is that why he swooped down to save you when you fell out of the nest? He did that off his own bat, you know.'

'Left it to the last minute, mind,' said Ronald.

'Well, yes. But it shows he cares.'

'Not that much. It's *you* he really loves. You know that.'

'OK, then, I'll take him home with me.'

'Really?'

'Yep. He can live in the stable with the donkey and the zebra. I think they'll just about all fit in. You can come and visit him. Uncle Rube's got my address.'

'But – when are you coming back?'

'That depends. When Uncle falls sick again, I suppose.'

'This is goodbye, then?' asked Ronald. He couldn't believe she was leaving, just like that. After all they had been through together.

'Yep,' said Hattie. 'I'm missing the animals. But I'll miss you too, Ron. Oh – just one thing before I go.'

'What?'

'Show us your Finger Sparkles.'

Ronald held up his sore, splinter-filled hands and

cleared his brain of all doubt. Confidence. That was the thing.

*'Inky Pinky Parkle, make my fingers sparkle!'*

And they did! A great explosion of green sparkles came streaming from the very tips of his fingers! They reached as far as the ornamental fountain. They were the best he'd ever managed. He'd have to try them out on the gargoyle in the archway.

He let them run for a bit, then dropped his hands, which tingled, but in a *good* way.

'That was pretty impressive,' said Hattie.

'Thanks,' said Ronald happily. 'I'll do a Fireball if you like.'

'Save it for the next time. I'm off. Try to keep your room tidy. When you get your new gear, put your old stuff in the bin. Bye, Ron.'

'Bye, Hattie. Um – thanks.'

'You're welcome. Don't forget to write to your aunty.'

'I will,' said Ronald. 'I *will*.'

He stood and watched her walk away.

'Bye, Denzil!' he called, as she reached the archway. 'Be a good boy!'

Denzil turned around and gave him a long, hard, yellow stare. Was that a wink? Was it? Or did he just have something in his eye? Hard to say. Then he turned and waddled after Hattie. A faint, rude odour of noxious gas came back on the breeze – and was gone.

Ronald stood in his turret room. It was all shipshape again. Hattie must have been up sorting it while he was away in Sludgehaven. The bedspread was washed, and a new rug replaced the old one. The coal was in the fireplace, where it belonged. The logs were in a tidy pile. The only clue that Denzil had ever been there was his empty basket.

Ronald couldn't bear to look at it.

Down in the lobby, Old Crabbit was standing on a stepladder, giving Mervyn his new coat of gold paint. Brenda was back at the reception desk, on the phone to Pauline.

'Back at work, I see, Crabbit!' called Ronald. He paused with the basket in his hand. 'Knee better, is it?'

'Yes,' mumbled Crabbit. 'It's fine.'

'Well, don't overdo it. You're looking a bit pale, I think.'

'I'm fine.'

'I hope you're not sickening for something.'

'I'm *fine*,' said Old Crabbit testily.

'Well, if you feel it's all getting too much, I suggest

you go back to the doctor. Get another sick note. Oh! I've just noticed! Isn't that the beginnings of a rash on your neck?'

'Eh?' Old Crabbit looked startled. His hand went to his neck.

'I'm pretty sure it *is*, you know,' said Ronald. 'Looks quite nasty. Oh – when you've finished painting, get rid of this, would you?' He set down the basket next to Mervyn. 'Be careful how you pick it up. Don't want you to put your back out again. And I'd be grateful for Hattie's address. I forgot to give her some money. And I want to send her some flowers. She's looking after my Dragon for me.'

And with that, he marched off down the corridor, following the delicious smell of frying fish, tossing his bulging purse from hand to hand and whistling as he went.

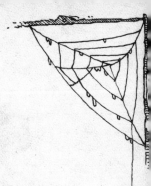

So. The End. It always arrives so quickly,
doesn't it?

TOO quickly in our opinion. So we've
decided to give you a sneak peek of the fast-talking,
drumstick-rolling, high-octane magical extravaganza that
is CRASH 'N' BANG

Turn over the page and all will be revealed . . .

For puzzles,
recipes and spells and
more from Kaye Umansky,
go to **www.pongwiffy.com**

# Chapter One

# *Filth*

'And where d'you think you're going?' enquired Witch Sludgegooey. Her head was deep in the oven at the time, but she still heard the door squeak.

'Rehearsal,' mumbled the small Fiend hovering on the doorstep. This was Filth, Sludgegooey's Familiar. He was clearly all set to go. Hair tuft gelled, nails painted black, desperate to be off and away.

'It's not Wednesday, is it?' Sludgegooey emerged from the oven with the tip of her hat on fire. She snatched it off and beat out the flames with a wet dishcloth.

'Extra one. Reviewing the pad.'

'That's musical language, is it? "Reviewing the pad"?'

'Yeah.'

'Meaning?'

'Making a list of what we play. Add some new tunes. Got to keep it fresh, man.'

'Don't call me *man*, Filth. Call me Mistress.'

'OK, Mistress.'

'Don't say OK. Say *yes*.'

'OK then, yeah. Yes.'

'How many times must I tell you? Familiars are supposed to speak *respectfully* to their Witches. Less of the slang. What time will you be back?'

'Dunno. I mean, not sure.'

'Because I could do with a bit of help clearing up.'

Sludgegooey flapped her dishcloth at the mountains of washing-up, deserts of spilt flour and oceans of slimy liquids that urgently awaited attention. She had been baking all day like a mad thing – not because she enjoyed it but because it was the Coven Cake Sale on Saturday. Of course, Filth should have helped, but he had been shut in his room with the radio on, seemingly deaf to her loud knockings and demands for assistance.

'Can't the Broom do it?' suggested Filth.

Sludgegooey's Broom tensed up in its corner, clearly not keen.

'It's too much for the Broom. It can't get inside the oven – it's the wrong shape.'

The Broom gave a sharp nod of agreement. It swept. It flew. It didn't do ovens.

'I'll do it,' promised Filth. 'Soon as I get back.'

'Ah, but *will* you?'

'For real. Yeah. I mean yes, Mistress.'

'Well – all right. But I want you back by midnight.'

'Cool.'

'It might be. I'd take a scarf. You can borrow my spotty one with the egg stain.'

'No, that's all right,' said Filth hastily. 'Look, I gotta split. Laters, yeah?'

'I *beg* your pardon?'

But Filth was already slouching off down the path, snapping his fingers, leaving Sludgegooey pondering once again on the wisdom of choosing a Fiend as a Familiar.

Of course, the real blame lay with the *Find A Familiar* catalogue, which had overstocked on Fiends and was promoting them heavily at the time. They had been described in glowing terms, as follows:

## *FIENDS*

*Whizzy, busy little helpers who run around chattering and cooking and putting shelves up whilst you, the Witch, relax on the sofa eating biscuits. Good value on the domestic front. Excellent DIY skills. Trained to assist in all areas of Magic including Incantations,*

*Cauldron Dancing and Herb Recognition. Next-day delivery.* OFFER OF THE MONTH! GET YOURS NOW!

Sludgegooey wasn't domestic and loved slumping around on sofas scoffing biscuits, so that appealed. But it was the *offer of the month* bit that did it because, like all Witches, she loved a bargain. She had sent off for one and waited excitedly for it to arrive and start cooking. She waited . . .

And waited . . .

And waited some more. Finally she complained to the catalogue company, who claimed to have dispatched one ages ago. The man on the phone was quite sniffy and wouldn't apologise, even when Sludgegooey threatened them with her latest curse – a particularly inventive one involving itchy ears, dreams featuring marzipan sharks and the weird smell of burning coming from your shoes.

The sniffy man remained firm. They'd sent one off. Not their fault it hadn't arrived. A bill was in the post.

Sludgegooey said she had no intention of coughing up for a Fiend she didn't have. The sniffy man referred her to the small print, which said she had to. Sludgegooey went into a sulk.

Then – finally – Filth showed up. He had no luggage other than a drum kit, stowed in a number of round boxes that he towed on a handcart. He didn't say where he'd been. When Sludgegooey demanded an explanation, he just shrugged and muttered something about having to see a dude about a thing, then asked to see his bedroom, which he immediately set about painting black and covering with music posters.

That had been a long time ago. And he hadn't changed.

In vain Sludgegooey waited for Filth to whizz, but he didn't. He stood around and leaned against things. He didn't scuttle, he sauntered. He didn't chat, he mumbled. He wasn't at all domestic and his DIY skills were non-existent. You couldn't trust him with the Magical stuff either. He was usually found collapsed in a chair, tapping out rhythms with his eyes closed while cakes caught fire, shelves collapsed and the Brew he was supposed to be watching boiled away to nothing.

He forgot the words to incantations. When he danced round the cauldron, he always added little improvisations of his own, which mucked up the recipe. He got all the herbs wrong because his mind was elsewhere. No, he wasn't a great Familiar. But . . .

Despite everything, Sludgegooey was fond of him.

And secretly rather proud. After all, no other Witch could boast of having a Familiar in an actual band.

'Remember me to the Boys!' she shouted as he disappeared into the trees. She felt a bit rotten about giving him a hard time. She knew he lived for rehearsals. He couldn't wait to be reunited with his drum kit, which he wasn't allowed to keep in the cottage. He would have liked to rehearse every night, but Sludgegooey drew the line at that. As she told him, being a Familiar is not a part-time job. She got tired of making excuses for him in front of the other Witches, who felt she should get a better grip. But . . .

She was fond of him. And she didn't want to stifle his creativity. For when Filth played the drums, he became – well, *Fiendish*. He sparkled. He shone. He whacked, he tapped, he boomed, he smashed, he juggled with his drumsticks. He exploded with rhythm and energy. He was on fire. As Sludgegooey said to a friend of hers, if only he put that amount of effort into his other duties, she'd be laughing.

He didn't, though. The friend had been quick to point that out. The friend had gone on to say other negative things about the wisdom of choosing a Fiend for a Familiar. She was that sort of friend. But then, *her* Familiar was a Hamster, so what did she know?